OTHERLIFE

LYNETTE DEVRIES

DIAMOND LIL PRESS

Cover design by Hannah DeVries.
Black and white cover illustration by Ava DeVries.
Professional editing by Red Circle Ink Editing.

Follow Lynette DeVries on Facebook, Instagram and Twitter, or visit www.authorlynettedevries.wordpress.com.

If you discover a typo or formatting issues, please contact lddevries@comcast.net so that it may be corrected.

DIAMOND LIL PRESS

ACKNOWLEDGMENTS

I am so lucky to have two daughters who always support my creative endeavors *and* were willing to contribute their talents and energy to the cover of this book. Ava captured the essence of *OtherLife* with her unique and haunting drawing style, and Hannah took my seed of an idea and cultivated it to capture the story's vibe.

I am thankful for the love and support of my husband, Derek, who tells a spine-tingling tale that ranks up there with my dad's *Legend of Lost Lake* saga and the colorful campfire orations of our friend, Laurence (of *Wiley & the Hairy Man* fame).

Special thanks for the priceless mentoring of author Anthea Lawrence, the editing magic of Jessa Slade at Red Circle Ink, the proofreading prowess of Ginger Lawrence, the support of beta readers Sydney Petranchuk and Ava DeVries, and the gorgeous photography of Daria Shevtsova.

～

For Chrissy,
who really gets me,
and with whom I share childhood memories
of an old house inhabited by carved birds
and perhaps a ghost or two.

PROLOGUE

Sometimes she walked the empty halls in human form.

It grounded her to fake the weight of gravity, to go through the motions. She didn't really expect to find him here, but each homecoming brought the pain back into sharp focus. The pain wasn't real, but it was better than nothing.

Nothingness was worse than death itself.

Today she chose to let the air currents carry her instead, to rise above the clumsy noise of earth. Maybe a different view would allow her to find an opening—a crack in the veneer between this world and that one, a way back to him.

She lit on the branch of a grand maple, a tree as old and stubborn as she was. From here, she could see the turret, its curtains drawn shut. That window had once given her a view of her forbidden love—the young lighthouse keeper who had promised her a better life. In the end, he hadn't been able to save her or their wee son.

A gust of wind, tinged with the promise of spring, whispered through the oak, riffling its new leaves. She didn't fight it. She rode the current up and away.

That's when she spotted it: an opening.

It wasn't a conscious offering—more like a fleeting yawn, a momentary lapse. The source was young, just as she had been when her life had ended. Young, and in a great deal of pain.

She zipped into the other dimension with raptor intensity, before it was too late. Her piercing cry was bird-song to anyone within earshot, but it was really more than that.

It was a prayer of thanksgiving, and a promise to give as much as she took.

1

Lucy McGowen had a unique skill set.

She could identify any bird—by Latin name and genus—simply by its call.

She could fill a blank notebook page with original song lyrics during a thirty-minute lunch period.

She blended easily with the hordes roaming the halls at Harborview High, using fashion the way a bird uses its plumage as camouflage. Her long, auburn hair set her apart from the crowd, but she somehow managed to stay well beyond the reaches of drama and conflict. She was liked but not popular.

She never cried.

Well, *almost* never.

This morning, her reflection glowered at her from the bathroom mirror, hair matted on one side, bloodshot eyes brimming with tears. She was tempted to look away. Her mom had always told her that excessive shows of emotion were a sign of weakness—but damn, it hurt.

She closed the bathroom door, desperate to be alone with her misery and shame.

She had gone to bed with the pain, which seemed to originate somewhere in her lower right jaw. She had killed the last of a bottle of ibuprofen to reduce the ache to a dull roar, but it was back again, louder than ever. It was a bone-deep pain that had wormed its way into her dreams until it had finally dragged her out of sleep.

Lucy had a high tolerance for pain—another of Joanne's claims—but she felt her limits being tested. She wandered downstairs, her palm pressed to the side of her face.

She hesitated at the kitchen doorway, greeted only by the smell of brewed coffee. She knew her mom was already perched at her laptop in her home office, just as she was most mornings by eight o'clock, weekends included.

Joanne was one of the top realtors in their sleepy seaport town of Portsmouth, New Hampshire. It was one of the oldest towns in the country, settled in the early sixteen-hundreds—a fact that Joanne flaunted as a perk for potential homebuyers.

It was early May, which meant Joanne had likely gotten up with the birds. For most folks in town, the spring thaw brought the promise of summer leisure, a slowing down, but the warming temperatures only intensified Joanne's focus. The barren trees turned plump and green, the frosty chill gave way to breezes scented by lilac blossoms and charcoal grills, and Joanne doubled down her efforts.

She had ninety days of prime showing time before the maples and birches hinted at autumn color, and she wouldn't waste a moment of them. Once the nights turned frosty again, she'd be forced to switch tactics—to highlight the nearby apple orchards and cozy fireplaces—and distract buyers from the hibernation imposed by the looming darkness of winter.

Lucy hesitated outside her mom's office door, weighing her options. She knew Joanne had a big open house today at one of her hottest properties, an eighteenth-century carriage house on Myrtle Street. Her nerves had been frayed all week, but today she would be in rare form.

She heard her mom talking on the phone. Judging by the number of F-bombs she was dropping, Lucy guessed the person on the other end was her young assistant, Nora. With her clients, Joanne was pure saccharine.

"The house may be ancient, Nora, but that doesn't mean it should smell ancient. Light some candles, open some windows and air that shit out."

Lucy considered retreating—her mom's mood was worse than she'd expected—but the wooden floor creaked beneath her feet. Joanne swiveled in her chair and raised a finger—a promise or a warning, Lucy wasn't sure which.

"Dig up that old-world-charm playlist, too— dulcimers and fiddles, you know the one? These people want quaint, we'll give them quaint."

Joanne turned her back to Lucy again. After a

moment, she sighed. "Yep—I should be there in two hours, tops."

She hung the phone up but made no move to turn around. Lucy wondered if she remembered she was standing there at all.

"Mom?" She cringed the moment it was out. Her mother had never actually gone by that nickname. She'd established her preference for being called by her first name when Lucy had spoken her first words.

She blamed the slip-up on her pain, a momentary glitch of her addled brain.

Joanne seemed too distracted to notice. She grunted, coffee cup lifted to her lips, but she still hadn't bothered to face her. "What's up, Luce?"

"My jaw feels worse." Lucy was careful to keep her tone matter-of-fact and free of self-pity. Whining—especially first thing in the morning—never failed to rub Joanne the wrong way. Whining was synonymous with weakness.

Joanne's hands floated over her laptop keys, her nails clattering. Her sigh was half-hearted.

She stopped typing to flap a hand in Lucy's direction. "Go find some Tylenol or something."

Lucy stood there another moment, waiting for more, but the keyboard attack resumed.

Reading between the lines was another skill Lucy had learned early on. Her mom's body language was loud and clear: *fend for yourself, kid.*

Lucy spent the next twenty minutes in a one-handed scavenger hunt, her other hand cradling her right cheek.

She found the elusive bottle of Tylenol in the back of a bathroom closet, on a shelf that served as a graveyard for half-used hair product rejects. Based on the well-worn label, the Tylenol had expired three years ago, but she was desperate.

She shook two white tablets into the palm of her hand, her eyes blurred with tears, then coaxed a third tablet out. She hadn't expected Joanne to pause her work to help her, but a little concern—or at least the pretense of it—would have been nice.

She swallowed the pills, then coughed when a voice boomed from the doorway.

"Hey, Goose." Lucy's dad, Jeremy, grinned at her, and she couldn't help but return the smile. He'd been calling her Goose for as long as she could remember—a carry-over of the childhood nickname Lucy Goosey.

"Hey." She averted her eyes, an effort to hide her deteriorating mood.

"You good?"

Lucy noted his wide eyes, the slight nod of his head meant to encourage cooperation. When Joanne was tense, Jeremy was tense, too. He was an airline pilot by trade, but on days like this—open house days—he made it his mission to keep the peace.

She thought about lying. It would be easier to nod, to say that everything was fine. But she was sleep-deprived, and the jaw pain had squashed the last of her pride.

"I've been better," she admitted.

Her dad made a face and took a small step backward. "Uh oh. Girl stuff?"

Lucy rolled her eyes and sighed. Jeremy could handle just about anything the Universe threw his way—he was a master at cockpit trouble-shooting—but *girl stuff* was beyond his scope.

He scratched the back of his neck. "Your mom's got a lot going on, but maybe she—"

"It's not that!" Lucy hadn't meant to yell, and she paused to reign in her emotions. "It's my jaw, Dad. It hurts so freaking bad."

Jeremy held a hand up, a gesture meant to hush her. "Sorry, Goose. I didn't know."

Lucy exhaled loudly. "I was hoping it would be better this morning." She hated the sound of her voice, fretful and apologetic. She hated feeling this needy.

Jeremy reached out to lay a hand on her shoulder. "Hey, don't worry. We'll get this taken care of, you and me."

He glanced at his watch and frowned, as though he was hoping to find a solution there instead of the time. "Hmmm. I'm on short call today."

Lucy was well-versed in airline crew lingo. As a reserve pilot on short call, her dad might get a call from crew scheduling any moment, and they could require him to sign in at the airport in as few as two hours.

She massaged the side of her face and wondered when the Tylenol might start to kick in. "Don't even think about asking Mom."

Jeremy flicked his eyes toward Joanne's office. "No chance." He bent to look into Lucy's eyes. "It's bad, huh?"

Lucy swallowed against the apology that was trying to bubble up and out of her. "It really is."

He clapped his hands together, his mind made up. "Okay, Goose. Let me jump in the shower. Call Dr. Nelson at Healthy Smiles—the number's in my phone contacts. See if they can squeeze us in. Tell them it's an emergency."

Lucy's eyes welled with fresh tears—a mixture of gratitude and guilt. "And if they call you out on a trip?"

Her dad shrugged. "I'll bring my flight bag and uniform in the car, just in case."

FIFTEEN MINUTES LATER, JEREMY HESITATED BESIDE THE car, jingling the keys, a question on his face.

Lucy's sixteenth birthday had come and gone, but she'd only logged a couple of hours of driving practice with her dad—most of them limited to abandoned parking lots.

She shook her head. "I don't think I'm up for it today, Dad."

Her dad bobbed his head. "Right." He opened the car door and slid into the driver's seat. "Don't worry, Goose. We'll get you there before too long."

There it was again—the tone that Lucy had been hearing in her dad's voice more and more lately. Beneath the false cheer, it was all guilt and resignation.

Lucy had overheard her parents arguing the day before. The wall between their rooms had muffled most of their fight, but she had managed to pick out one damning proclamation by Joanne: "If you think it's so important for her to get her license, Jer, make it happen! This whole thing was your idea in the first place!"

Lucy's thoughts had swarmed around that statement like ants to a crumb. What whole thing?

Their marriage?

Motherhood?

Now Lucy collapsed into the passenger seat and glanced at her dad. She saw the serious set of his jaw and sighed.

"It's not your fault, Dad," she said, and she meant it.

Her dad traveled a lot—about half of the month, thanks to his airline flying schedule and the commute that required him to drive an hour to Boston—and when he was home, he tended to all things domestic.

Joanne was the queen of staging homes for sale, but she didn't have the time or energy to keep their own home in order. She had a keen eye for well-appointed kitchens, but Lucy couldn't remember the last time Joanne had cooked an actual meal for their family.

When Jeremy started the car, the radio blasted them with the sounds of AC/DC—loud enough to vibrate the seats. Lucy clapped her hands over her ears, her tooth pain forgotten.

Her dad reached out and killed the music. "Sorry, Goose. It's a long drive from Boston—helps me stay awake."

"I think you have hearing damage, Dad. All those years of jet engine noise."

Jeremy chuckled. "Hey, that commute is my only shot at a musical escape."

Lucy snorted. "You call that music?"

Jeremy grinned. "You wouldn't know good music if it bit you," he said. "Just like your mom."

Lucy looked out the window, her lips pressed together, tormented by the truth tickling the back of her throat. She'd been drawn to music as a small child, but her mother had always insisted that time spent on idle distractions—especially creative ones—was wasted time. Creativity hadn't made Joanne the number one realtor; hard work had.

Lucy had a childhood memory of languishing in the bathtub, where the acoustics were perfect for singing the morning song her kindergarten teacher greeted them with. Her mom had appeared in the doorway, the phone cradled against her shoulder, a finger pressed to her lips to shush her. Lucy had climbed out of the tub, tears stinging her eyes, her song snuffed out by shame.

A year ago, everything had changed.

Lucy had stumbled upon a battered, badly tuned guitar at a garage sale. She paid five dollars for it, then tucked it beneath her bed when she got home. Once she had the house to herself, she pulled it out and strummed it.

The sound had awakened something inside her.

After that, whenever she was home alone—which was the case more often than not—she worked on learning the chords to her favorite songs.

At first, she'd only hummed the melodies, the notes a

whisper in her throat. Before long she was singing the lyrics in full voice, the hairs on her own arms standing up. Composing her own songs—and scribbling the lyrics down as they came to her—felt as natural as breathing. She felt like a sorceress stumbling upon a secret stash of magic potions and spells.

"I know more than you think," Lucy said, then avoided her dad's inquisitive gaze. For months, she'd been tempted to reveal this secret side of herself to her dad—and today, pain had her defenses lowered—but she thought better of it. Once Jeremy knew about her singing, Joanne would know, and she couldn't risk the sting of disapproval.

Not today, when the pain had her so close to breaking down.

"You don't have to pretend, Goose," Jeremy said. He reached over and patted her knee. "I know you're hurting."

Lucy heard the unspoken message beneath his words: *I'm not like your mother.*

She tried to smile. "Thanks for taking me today, Dad."

Jeremy fell silent, and Lucy waited for her heartbeat to slow to a march. Her musical secret was safe—at least, for now.

At that moment, as her entire lower jaw throbbed in time with her pulse, she couldn't imagine ever feeling good enough to speak a full sentence, let alone sing an entire song. The Tylenol hadn't even touched the pain.

Lucy's phone dinged with a text notification—the

third one in the last half hour. One glance at her phone screen confirmed what she already knew. The messages were all from her boyfriend, Nate Mills, and they would keep coming unless she responded.

Nate was kind and sensitive—an open book, emotion-ally—and he doted on Lucy with a fervor that bordered on fanaticism. He seemed to have one singular mission: to explore her feelings as though she were a rare bird on the verge of extinction.

There was a part of Lucy that envied Nate's vulnera-bility, that wanted to mirror his emotional honesty. The part of her that had learned to keep herself closed off—who had retreated into silence after her mom shushed her—was stronger. There was no room for weakness in Joanne's house—or in Lucy's life.

She ignored the phone on her lap.

Her dad shot her a quizzical look. "Nate the Great?"

She shrugged and leaned her head back against the car seat. "That's a very bold guess."

Jeremy chuckled beside her. "Can't blame the kid for having good taste, can you?"

Lucy blinked at her dad, bemused. She pressed her fingers to her cheek, the only barrier between the outside world and the five-alarm fire ravaging her lower gumline.

Her dad was right—Nate *was* a great person, which made her a heartless jerk for taking him for granted.

"He can be a little intense sometimes," she confided. There it was—the inevitable twinge of guilt.

"I don't mind if you text him back." Her dad made it a point to keep his eyes on the road, but Lucy had heard the accusation in his tone. He clearly thought she was being mean.

"I can barely think straight right now, Dad," Lucy huffed. "I don't think I've ever had this much pain in my entire life."

"I know, Goose."

Lucy spent the next several minutes compiling a mental list of all the reasons she shouldn't text Nate back.

First and foremost, responding to his repeated texts would only encourage him.

Also, just because she had a cell phone with her didn't mean she was obligated to use it. It was a device, not a leash.

She also suspected that any response she might summon now—when she was feeling this salty—would do more harm than good. She didn't want to hurt his feelings any more than she already had.

"It isn't like we've gone days without talking." She spoke this defense aloud, and Jeremy glanced at her, his eyebrows arched.

"Yeah?"

"We talked before bed last night," she continued. "I'm not playing hard to get. I'm not—" Lucy let her voice trail off, but her dad flicked his eyes at her, proof that he'd read between the lines. *I'm not like Mom.*

"I get it, Goose." Her dad had slipped into his soothing hostage negotiator voice—the one he used with Joanne all the time. "Let's worry about you right now."

2

The receptionist at the front desk seemed to interpret the scowl on Lucy's face.

She turned to Jeremy, eyes wide, and handed him a clipboard. "Just need you to update your insurance info and whatnot," she said. "And give consent for today's treatment."

Lucy followed her dad to a row of chairs at the back of the waiting room, determined to ignore the droning of an unseen instrument in the next room. She'd never been a fan of dental offices—or the way you couldn't seem to leave one without your mouth hanging slack or your jaw aching from being propped open like a screen door on a breezy day. She hated the humiliation of having her saliva —and her Novocaine-numbed tongue—sucked up by the hygienist's tube.

Her dad hunched over the forms on the clipboard, his pen scratching at the pages faster than he could possibly read them.

Lucy gave her dad a dubious look. "Jeez. That's a lot of fine print. It's like you're buying a house or something."

Jeremy peered at her over his reading glasses. "Liability purposes," he assured her. "They have to mention all the risks, no matter how unlikely."

A repetitive buzzing interrupted Jeremy's box-checking.

"Shit," he breathed. He reached for his back pocket and drew his cell phone out. "It's crew scheduling."

Jeremy handed Lucy the clipboard, then ducked out the waiting room door and into the hall.

The receptionist looked up at Lucy. "Finished with your paperwork, hon?"

Lucy scanned the forms—her dad had signed and dated everything—and stood up. "I think so."

Jeremy came back into the waiting room, frowning. "I was afraid this might happen."

Lucy dragged her eyes between her dad and the receptionist, who was watching them with a half-smile.

"They assigned you?" Lucy hated her frantic tone, but pain had brought her feelings close to the surface. She despised dental work, but the thought of leaving this office without relief was a thousand times worse.

"I'm sorry." Jeremy ran a hand through his hair. He glanced at his phone and muttered under his breath. Lucy knew from experience that he was making a mental calculation of how much time he had to get from their New Hampshire town to the airport in Boston. It was a one-hour drive in good traffic.

He looked up and sighed. "Just enough time to get there and change into my uniform if I leave right now."

"Go, Dad. I'm fine," Lucy insisted.

Jeremy bent to look into her eyes. "Okay, Goose. Loved you before and I'll love you after."

Lucy managed a smile. "And all the days in between." Her response was automatic.

"Lucy?" A dark-haired dental hygienist had appeared in the doorway.

Lucy's jaw clenched involuntarily, and she winced. She raised her hand up. "Coming."

Jeremy glanced at his phone again. "I'll text your mom and let her know I had to go," he said. "She won't mind picking you up when you're done."

Lucy heard the doubt in his voice. Her mom was probably setting up for her open house at this very moment. Only a natural disaster could divert her attention from that open house.

"Okay, yeah." Lucy didn't want to add to her dad's stress. He had a long drive ahead of him and a 757 full of passengers to deal with. She didn't want him wasting his mental energy on her toothache. "I'll be fine. Go, Dad. I don't want you to be late."

Jeremy put his hands on Lucy's shoulders and looked into her eyes. He was a walking contradiction; he loved being an airline pilot, but he hated leaving home. He seemed to sense that his absence left their home open to strained silences and tension, as if he were the glue that held them all together.

"Love you, Goose." He planted a kiss on her forehead. "I'll text you after I talk to your mom."

Lucy backed toward the hygienist who was waiting for her in the hallway. "Love you, too, Dad. Be safe."

She could feel her dad's eyes on her back as she turned to follow the hygienist down the hall. In another five minutes, he would steer his car onto the south ramp for Interstate 95 bound for Logan International.

"How's your day so far?" The hygienist flashed a smile over her shoulder.

Lucy considered telling her the truth—that it was a steaming pile of crap—but she forced a smile. "Good."

DR. NELSON HAD JUST TOUCHED HIS STEEL INSTRUMENT to one of Lucy's back molars when she heard a buzz. The timing made her think of the game Operation, and she had the improbable urge to laugh.

"You're very popular this morning," the doctor said under his breath. He was referring to the buzz, the third one since Lucy had settled into the padded dental chair. She was so accustomed to Nate's frequent check-ins that she hardly flinched at the text tones, but it seemed the rest of the world found them impossible to ignore.

Lucy waited for the doctor to withdraw his instrument. "Sorry." She considered texting Nate back—a quick reassurance to appease him—or powering her phone off altogether. She was still waiting for her dad to tell her he'd gotten ahold of Joanne, a parental passing of the baton. As much as she hated the thought of her dentist getting distracted while he was wrist-deep in her mouth, she wanted her dad to be able to reach her.

The dentist glanced at the monitor beside him, where her dental x-rays were on display. Lucy had already spotted the dark blob on the lower right quadrant, but she hadn't asked the dentist about it. She had a feeling he was about to tell her more than she needed to know about her problem and the solution, which would probably involve jaw clamps and drilling.

She thought about her dad, who was probably halfway to Boston by now, and she had the impulse to jump out of the chair and thank the doctor for his time. Maybe the pain wasn't so bad after all.

"Well, young lady, you were very smart to come in today," the doctor said. It was as if he'd read her mind and sensed she needed a pep talk. "Unfortunately, you have a fairly serious tooth infection with an abscess in the tissues below. It appears the infection has already infiltrated the bone, and without immediate intervention . . ." He locked eyes with the dental hygienist sitting on the other side of Lucy, leaving her to fill in the blanks.

Without immediate intervention—what? Brain damage?

Death?

She dragged her eyes back to the x-ray on the screen. When she swallowed, she registered the faint taste of blood, no doubt from Dr. Nelson's gum prodding.

"So, what now?" She turned to the hygienist, who seemed like a reasonable person. "Take some heavy-duty antibiotics?"

The hygienist's blue mask hid her smile, but her eyes crinkled. Lucy wasn't sure if she was smiling with amusement or compassion; both would have annoyed her if she wasn't at their complete mercy.

Dr. Nelson cleared his throat and patted her arm. "I'm afraid we're going to need to be more aggressive than antibiotics," he said. "An abscess can lead to sepsis."

Lucy wasn't sure what sepsis was, but based on Dr. Nelson's no-nonsense tone, it wasn't good.

She shrugged, but her heart had kicked into a gallop inside her rib cage. "Okay."

This was the part where Lucy imagined most kids would defer to a parent—one who would ideally be seated nearby, or at least no farther than the waiting room.

"In some cases a root canal would be the next step, but I'm afraid something this involved requires a full extraction."

Lucy made an involuntary sound—a cross between a sigh and a whimper. She saw the doctor flick his eyes at the hygienist.

"Extraction?" Lucy asked. "As in pulling the tooth out?" She brought a protective hand to her cheek. "I should probably call my parents and check with them."

Translation: I did not sign up for this.

"Of course," the hygienist chimed in. Lucy thought she detected a note of pity in her voice. "We'll be back in a minute or two." She nodded at the doctor, and they left Lucy alone in the space-age torture chamber, surrounded by sterile instruments.

Lucy drew in a deep breath, then let it seep out. She dialed her dad first—he was far more likely to answer a call from her, even if he was making a mad dash through the airport—but after eight rings, she hung up.

She dialed her mom, rehearsing her mental script: *they want to yank my tooth out—please please get me out of this!*

After the first ring, a text message from Joanne came through: *Knee-deep in this open house!! What's up?*

Lucy closed her eyes against the tears burning in them. She composed a text with trembling fingers. *Tooth infection. Doc wants to pull the tooth out!!*

She added a single word after that—*scared!*—then deleted it.

She read her mom's response: *Okay! Text me when you're done and I'll send Nora to pick you up.*

Lucy dropped the phone on her lap, screen down, as if the inanimate object had let her down. She tilted her head back and stared at the monitor mounted from the ceiling. A slow-motion ballet of moon jellyfish had been playing on the screen all along. Lucy supposed it was meant to be soothing—and distracting—but the more she watched those jellies, the tighter her throat felt.

She was clearly on her own here.

"So?" The dental hygienist reappeared by her side, stretching a fresh pair of latex gloves over her fingers.

Lucy glanced over her shoulder at the hallway. Dr. Nelson wasn't back yet, but he would be any second. She envisioned herself bolting from the chair, away from those serene jellyfish, out into the sunny parking lot. She could catch an Uber and be home in twenty minutes.

The pulsating ache in her lower jaw intensified—a reminder that she had come here for a reason. Her problem wasn't going anywhere without serious intervention.

"Guess I don't really have a choice, huh?" She tried to chuckle, but her throat had gone dry and she coughed instead.

Dr. Nelson strode into the room, whistling. The hygienist nodded at him—some unspoken cue—and Lucy saw the look in her eyes. *We've got a nervous one,* that look said. *Handle with care.*

The doctor turned to face Lucy and crouched beside her chair. She knew exactly what he was doing; he was coming down to her level, pretending they were playing for the same team. Lucy was freaked out, but she wasn't stupid—she and Dr. Nelson occupied different leagues altogether. He had complete power.

"Of course you have a choice," the doctor crooned. "You can always refuse treatment."

The hygienist nodded in agreement, but the eyes above the blue mask didn't lie. Refusing treatment would be unwise and highly unorthodox.

"And if I wait?" Lucy stared straight ahead, afraid to look at either of them.

The doctor motioned to the damning x-ray once again.

"Sepsis is no laughing matter," he said. "If the infection enters your bloodstream, it becomes a medical emergency."

The hygienist's unblinking eyes corroborated the

doctor's claims, and Lucy felt the truth settle over her like a poisonous fog. She needed to put her big-girl pants on, pronto.

"Okay," she said. It *wasn't* okay, but what choice did she have?

Her cell phone buzzed on her lap, making her arms twitch. A quick glance revealed the source of the text— Nate, of course—and she almost ignored it, the way she'd ignored all the others. She cupped it in her sweat-slicked palm.

"Can I send a quick text?" she asked.

The doctor patted her shoulder and nodded at the hygienist, who busied herself with preparations for the procedure.

They had likely assumed she was texting her parents —that she was a typical teenager, the kind with parents who were always within reach, at least by phone. They were wrong.

She didn't owe Nate the courtesy of a text, but she hoped it would make her feel better to tell someone— anyone—what she was up against. Just in case.

Hey. Having a tooth pulled. I'll call you later if everything goes okay.

She thought about changing that *if* to something less cryptic, then decided to leave it. It was a comfort to know someone out there would be sending her good thoughts, worrying about her.

She hit send, then powered her phone off. Her text would be like throwing fuel on a fire—the fire being Nate and his round-the-clock devotion to her. She didn't need her phone blowing up every thirty seconds while the doctor had his fat fingers in her mouth.

The dental hygienist had laid a disturbing number of gleaming instruments on the tray beside them. Lucy let her eyes slide over them briefly, then leaned back for a view of the jellyfish pulsating above her chair. She waited for her breathing to fall in line with those jellies in their hypnotic dance, but the more she tried to control it, the less she could.

"Are you okay, hon?" The hygienist laid a gloved hand on her arm.

Lucy smiled and blinked tears away. "Fine." She swallowed against the choking sensation in her throat. "A little nervous, I guess."

"Perfectly understandable," the hygienist murmured.

Lucy closed her eyes and wondered if the woman behind the mask had children at home, and if she used the same soothing tone in the face of temper tantrums.

She wondered how that kind of nurturing might have shaped Lucy during her formative years, then realized it didn't matter. She'd grown up with a dad whose job took him away for half the month and a mother who favored work over family time. Lucy had taught herself to ride a bike, how to mend a tear with a needle and thread, how to get herself to the bus stop. The arrangement had allowed her room to grow and breathe without interference.

Lucy thought she would do just about anything for some interference right now.

Dr. Nelson reappeared by her side with a syringe.

Lucy averted her eyes—was he smiling or frowning behind his surgical mask?—and decided to give those gliding jellyfish another chance.

The shot didn't feel good, but it wasn't as bad as Lucy had expected.

By the time Dr. Nelson returned to check on her numbness, the throbbing ache that had dominated the last twenty-four hours had quieted some.

"How're we doing?" The doctor peered at her over his glasses, which had microscope lens attachments affixed to them. "Should be good and numb by now."

Lucy shrugged. "I think so."

The doctor prodded her lower gum, and she winced.

"You can feel that?" He seemed surprised—and maybe a little irritated.

Lucy put her hand on her chest. Beneath her rib cage, her heart was thundering.

"It's the epinephrine in the Novocaine shot," the hygienist said. "It can affect your heart rate. Not to worry, sweetie."

Lucy managed a lopsided smile and pointed at the ceiling. "The jellyfish aren't cutting it . . . do you have anything stronger?" It was a sad attempt at humor, but the nurse glanced at the doctor.

"More lidocaine . . . or CS?" she asked.

CS? Lucy scrambled to decipher that, but her mind could only come up with something irrational: *Call Security.*

"Is something wrong?" She tried to sound calm and coherent, but her enormous tongue wasn't cooperating.

The doctor shook his head. "Everything's fine, dear. Just need to make sure you're properly prepped, and we should have you out of here in a couple of hours."

Lucy sat forward in the chair, an involuntary revolt by her muscles. "A couple of hours?"

"The extraction will be somewhat involved, and then we'll have to clean the infection out of the underlying tissues, stitch things up, go over after-care . . ."

Lucy swung her legs over the side of the chair. Her earlier thoughts about freedom—about growth and self-sufficiency—were bullshit.

"I'm sorry," she mumbled. "I can't."

"We can offer conscious sedation," the hygienist offered.

Lucy blinked at her, mute with embarrassment. Ah, *conscious sedation,* otherwise known as CS.

She settled back into the chair and tried to still the trembling of her arms and legs. "What's that—like laughing gas?"

The doctor sighed, but Lucy tried not to take it personally. "We administer a sedative intravenously, and it does two things. It relaxes you—a lot—and it blocks pain."

Lucy blinked at him, hopeful. "Both good things."

The doctor's eyes crinkled at that. "Indeed. You'll need a ride home afterward, of course. And because you're a minor, we require parental permission."

Lucy's heart sank. One of her parents was in another state—or up in the air, headed far, far away. The other was only a few miles away, but she might as well be on another planet for all the good it did Lucy.

"Oh." When she remembered the sheaf of paperwork in the lobby, she perked up. "My dad signed a bunch of forms in the waiting room."

The doctor nodded at the hygienist, who disappeared for a minute, then returned.

"He signed a form allowing permission for any treatment, including conscious sedation." Her eyes dropped to Lucy's face again. "So unless you need to call him and check in . . ."

Lucy relaxed her grip on her armrests, where her hands had left oily handprints. She'd already endured thirty minutes of poking and prodding, not to mention a shot that had left her face feeling like a rubber mask. Her tooth infection was only going to get worse from here. Postponing the inevitable was pointless.

Her parents trusted her to make all kinds of decisions. Why was this any different?

Lucy clenched her teeth to silence the voice in her head. Her bite felt off, as though her teeth had undergone a seismic shift in the last half hour, but she knew it was just the anesthetic messing with her.

"No need to check in," she said. She felt a strange calm wash over her—another shift, this one a hundred percent mental. "Let's do this."

LUCY BARELY FLINCHED WHEN THE IV NEEDLE SLID INTO her arm. She wanted to believe it was because she was a badass, but she suspected she had the puff of nitrous oxide to thank for that.

She lay back in the chair, feeling like a passenger embarking on a space expedition. That's when it struck her: the jellyfish undulating above her weren't sea creatures at all. They were aliens, their glowing, translucent forms designed for zero gravity.

They beckoned for Lucy to follow them, up and away from the heaviness of planet earth—and so she did.

3

Lucy felt a gentle hand on her back.

The hand was making slow circles, round and round. She tried to follow that hand with her mind's eye, but just as she was getting the hang of it, the circles stopped altogether.

"Lucy?" The voice beside her belonged to a female, which was something of a shock. She'd assumed the person attached to the circling hand was Nate, the most touchy-feely person she knew. He claimed he'd always been a sucker for physical touch—that there was nothing a simple hug couldn't fix.

Lucy's parents were not physically demonstrative—she was more likely to get a high-five from her dad than a hug—so becoming Nate's girlfriend had been a tactile crash course.

The female voice came back, closer to her ear. "Can you open your eyes, baby?"

Lucy felt her forehead crinkle involuntarily. That voice was familiar, but the tone wasn't.

Where *was* she?

Why were her eyes closed, and who knew her well enough to call her baby?

Another voice chimed in nearby. "We had to use a fair amount, so it might take her a few minutes to come out of it. Take your time."

Lucy remembered now. She had come in to have her infected tooth taken care of. The pain was gone, like a deafening roar suddenly muted. It had left an emptiness behind—a blissful silence. She would never take the absence of pain for granted again.

"Better," Lucy tried to say, but her lips felt oversized and clumsy, and it came out wrong.

"Beer?" The person beside her chuckled, another clue. She'd heard that chuckle before, hadn't she? "It's not even five o'clock yet, baby."

Lucy fluttered her eyelids, afraid to ask too much of them all at once. She was greeted by a jarring, sideways view of a row of chairs, a floor the color of the ocean. It reminded her of the jellyfish that had escorted her through her ordeal and felt a sudden, irrational surge of emotion. She missed those jellyfish—and she hadn't had a chance to thank them or say goodbye.

"Her eyes are open," the beside-her voice said.

"She might be a little out of it for a bit, laughing or crying, or both," the other voice said. There was the squeaking of rubber soles on the floor. "She might say some crazy things. It's normal as the sedative wears off."

Lucy pushed herself into a sitting position, amazed by the effort it took. The room tilted with a sickening whoosh, then slowly settled. She'd never been drunk before, but she'd felt buzzed once at a party—the effects of a Jell-O shot handed to her by a well-meaning friend. It had made her feel fuzzy and off-balance—which was how she felt now.

She opened her mouth to speak, but her dead tongue rebelled.

A lady in rainbow-patterned scrubs approached her with a Dixie cup. "Here's some water." She turned to the woman beside Lucy. "It'll help move the sedative out of her system."

Lucy took the cup with a shaky hand and dribbled half of the water down the front of her shirt. She turned to the woman beside her with a smirk, then blinked at her, bewildered.

"Joanne!" she exclaimed. There was a wad of something packed into the pouch of her lower cheek, but she barely noticed.

"That's right." Her mom smiled as if Lucy had guessed the answer to a tricky trivia question. "Good job, baby."

"The gauze packing can come out in another hour," the rainbow lady said. She shuffled a stack of papers, then handed them to Joanne. "Here are the after-care instructions. Saltwater gargling, soft foods for a few days, pain medication as needed. It's all here, and if you have any questions—"

Lucy stared at her mom, the empty Dixie cup crumpled in her fist. "What happened?"

Joanne reached a hand out, and Lucy flinched.

"You had some dental work done—" She tucked a wisp of Lucy's hair behind her ear, an act that felt wildly out of character.

"No," Lucy protested. She jabbed at the gauze in her mouth with the tip of her tongue. "I mean, what are *you* doing here?"

Joanne made a quizzical face at the receptionist across the room, and Lucy saw the unspoken message there: *oh boy—my daughter is high as a kite!*

"How else would you get home, baby?" Joanne folded the after-care instructions into her purse. Lucy had never seen it before—it was a bag woven with multi-colored fibers, very different from the sleek black leather bag she normally carried.

She opened her mouth to speak, then closed it. Her head was throbbing, and she felt like she had to concentrate on staying upright. She didn't understand why her mom had changed her plans to send Nora to pick her up, or why she was calling her baby, but those questions could wait.

"My head hurts," she said.

The receptionist looked up from her computer work. "Some people have mild headaches as the sedative wears off. Would you like some Tylenol?"

Joanne flashed her a smile. "I have some right here," she said.

Lucy watched as her mom opened her bag and sorted through its contents—first-aid kit, granola bars, sunglasses case, and a small, spiral-bound notebook embellished with sequins. Joanne found the Tylenol, shook two out, and went to the water cooler to fill another Dixie cup.

Lucy watched her go, dazed, then dropped her eyes to that sequined notebook.

"What's that?" she asked, pointing.

Her mom handed her the water and chuckled. "It's my book of inspirations, remember?" She gave Lucy a funny look—a look that hinted at worry—then zipped her bag. "For jotting down ideas as they come to me."

Lucy stared at her mom, dumbstruck.

Whatever they had given her hadn't just numbed the right half of her face—it had coated her brain in a thick sludge. Maybe things would make more sense later, when it had fully worn off.

Until then, she would keep her questions to herself.

4

Lucy didn't think to turn her phone back on until they were turning onto their street.

She could only imagine the backlog of texts from Nate, especially after the dubious message she'd sent just before powering it off.

When she reached for her back pocket, she found it empty. "My phone!"

Joanne glanced at her and smiled. "It's in my purse, baby. You gave it to me for safekeeping before they called you back, remember?"

Lucy considered that for a moment, her mind circling back to the moments before her dental procedure. Her dad had been called away on a trip, and she had been alone after that. Alone with nothing but her own, frantic thoughts and those serene jellyfish for company.

Hadn't she?

"Ella was sweet enough to keep Maggie overnight,"

her mom said. "Early morning appointments are hard enough without that chaos, right?"

Lucy's head felt like it was filled with cement. She leaned it against the headrest and frowned. "Who's Maggie? And what about your open house?"

Her lower gums and jaw were starting to come alive again, a strange tingling sensation as the last of the numbness wore off.

Joanne slowed the car to a stop in their driveway, then gave her an odd look. "Let's get you inside, huh? Maybe you can take a nap and sleep off the rest of that sedative."

Lucy watched her mom rummage in her bag until she found her cell phone. She handed it over with a smile.

"Thanks for picking me up," she said, unbuckling her seat belt. "You really didn't have to."

Joanne's chuckle was uneasy. "Of course I did. You didn't think I was going to make you hitchhike home, did you?"

Lucy blinked hard to clear her eyes and her mind. She wanted to ask her mom more questions—whether she'd cut her open house short or if Nora was handling it—but she was overcome by exhaustion.

She heaved the passenger door open and got out of the car, feeling like she'd just endured a triathlon instead of a dental procedure.

She expected to hear Joanne's car pulling back out of the driveway—with Nora's no-nonsense voice already booming over the car's Bluetooth speaker—but she heard the other car door slam.

She turned to see her mom coming up the front walk behind her. Lucy's eyes dropped to Joanne's flowing, wide-leg pants—a wild swing from the business suits she usually wore to open houses—and she stopped in her tracks.

Joanne patted her on the side of the face as she went around her to unlock the front door. It appeared she had no intention of going anywhere—or explaining why she'd bailed on the open house she'd been hyper-focused on for weeks.

Lucy dimly registered the new details as she followed her mom inside—the cheerful tulips in the window box, the eucalyptus wreath on the front door—but it would take all of her energy to haul herself up the stairs toward her waiting bed. She would sleep now, and she would sort everything out after.

Moments later, as she drifted off, she heard her mom whistling a nameless tune downstairs. It should have been a comfort, but instead it left her arms stippled with goosebumps.

LUCY WOKE TO THE RHYTHMIC BUZZING OF HER CELL phone.

It took her a moment to get her bearings: she was in her own bed, and the clock on her nightstand claimed it was 1:11 p.m. Her eyes were bleary from sleep, but the numbness had lifted and her headache was gone.

Her mouth felt much better, too—although a cautious bite down reminded her that her cheek was still packed with a wad of gauze. She spit it out and cringed.

"Gross." Her voice came out as a raspy croak.

She gathered up her cell phone and sighed. She felt like a jerk for leaving Nate out of the loop for so many hours—for letting him worry longer than he needed to. She was amazed that he hadn't just shown up on her doorstep when his texts went unanswered.

She went to her text messages and scrolled down, then up again, her mind struggling to make sense of what she saw on her screen. She didn't see Nate's latest text.

In fact, she didn't see *any* of his texts. The text string between the two of them stretched back months—a chronological, abbreviated diary of their relationship— but she couldn't find it.

"What the hell?" She pushed herself up off the bed and gathered air in her lungs as she yanked her bedroom door open. "Joanne?"

An unfamiliar smell met her at the top of the stairs. She scrunched her face up, sniffing, then registered what it was. Someone was cooking.

She hurried down the stairs, her hand sliding along the banister. The weird, heavy sludge had left her head, but she felt shaky with anger. "Joanne!"

She found her mom at the stove, her head bent as she busied herself with whatever was sizzling in the pan. When Joanne turned to smile at her, Lucy took the details in with a single glance—Hard Rock Cafe T-shirt and leggings, neither of which she'd ever glimpsed before today.

"Feeling better, babe?"

Lucy nodded mutely, then let her eyes scan the kitchen. The counter was a riot of vegetable scrapings and measuring cups. She couldn't remember the last time she'd seen her mom cook something that didn't require a microwave. Lucy had become adept at foraging in the freezer and pantry, which were perpetually stocked with frozen entrees and ramen.

"What's all this?" she asked. She hadn't meant for it to sound like an accusation, but she supposed it was, in a way.

Joanne wrinkled her nose and laughed. "I believe there's a word for it . . . um . . . dinner?" She went back to her stirring. "Making a casserole. Your dad's on his way home as we speak."

Was *that* it?

Had Joanne and her dad had some kind of fight—and was this an attempt at an apology?

Then she remembered the cell phone violation that had sent her flying downstairs in the first place. She held her phone up and glared at her mom.

"Where'd it go?" she demanded.

Joanne raised an eyebrow at her and wiped her hands on a dish towel. "Where'd what go?"

Lucy huffed loudly and made her eyes big. "My conversation with Nate. There's a string of like a thousand texts, and they're all gone. Did you delete them while I was at the dentist or something?"

Joanne blinked at her, her smile faltering. After a

moment, she gingerly reached a hand out to touch Lucy's forehead.

"Are you feeling okay? The dentist said you might be a little off for a—"

"I feel fine," Lucy said. "You're the one who had my phone in your purse. If you didn't delete those texts, who did?"

Joanne held her hands up. "Slow down, baby," she said. "Who's Nate?" The smile returned to her mom's face. "Have you been talking to a boy?"

The genuine curiosity in her mom's eyes made Lucy take a step backward. She waited for Joanne to take it back—to admit she was just messing with her—but she only stared at Lucy, that hopeful grin on her face.

"Stop." Lucy barely recognized her own voice. "Joanne, please—just stop."

Her mom shook her head, her smile faded but not altogether gone. "What's this Joanne business? You may be sixteen, but I'm still your mother."

Lucy turned on her heels and bolted from the kitchen. She considered taking the stairs two at a time and diving back under the covers, then decided that wasn't far enough away.

She jerked the front door open and didn't stop running until she was at the end of her block, where her mom's baffled calls couldn't reach her anymore.

5

Lucy didn't realize where she was headed until she stood on the sidewalk in front of the Myrtle Street house.

The Victorian three-story home, built in the eighteen-hundreds, was Joanne's most prized listing. Lucy had seen the house in passing hundreds of times, but she'd never been inside it. She'd heard plenty about the interior from overheard snippets of phone conversations with prospective clients: original marble fireplaces, stately parlor and arched doorways, top-floor turret with full views of the Piscataqua River.

She wasn't thinking about those details now as she stood facing the house, her breath whistling in her throat, her heart racing. This was the site of Joanne's big open house—the one she'd insisted was her top priority just this morning.

The one that had demanded her full attention for the last several weeks.

Only now there was no hint of an open house—or the blue and white for-sale sign featuring Joanne's name or the logo of her company, Harbor Home Hunters.

On the color flyers Joanne had printed for the event, the house looked pristine-vintage. Now it appeared utterly abandoned. Overgrown lilac bushes flanked the front lawn and dusted the weedy lawn with purple blossoms. The paint on the weathered house was peeling, the faded roof still littered with cast-off oak leaves from last winter.

Carved wooden birds—some ornate, some rudimentary—were scattered about and affixed to the exterior. White painted gulls decorated the tops of the front porch railings, one on either side, a pair of watchful sentries. At the top of the turret, an osprey perched, the tip broken off of one of its outstretched wings, its eyes vacant. Her mom had never mentioned the carved birds before; it was a detail Lucy would have remembered.

She spun in a slow circle, her mind a dazed blank, surveying her surroundings. Maybe she was on the wrong street, at the wrong house. Maybe she was still feeling the after-effects of her dental sedation and had taken off in the wrong direction altogether. She faced the house again, hands on her hips.

The wooden numbers above the front door were missing, but she could see the faded outline where they once had been. She'd heard her mom recite the address dozens of times: 111 Myrtle Street.

This was the right house—but everything about it looked wrong.

Lucy felt her knees wobble, and she allowed gravity to

pull her into a crouch. She perched on the curb and tucked her arms over her stomach, which had been churning ever since she'd caught her mom in the improbable act of making dinner.

The cooking was weird enough, but the rest of it—the missing text string and Joanne's bizarre response to it—was incomprehensible. Lucy felt like the butt of an elaborate prank, but that didn't exactly fit. Her mom had never been one to joke about anything.

"Okay, you got me," Lucy said aloud, as if those magic words might somehow restore order to her world. Her voice came out high and shrill, but the simple act of speaking had given her an idea. Instead of sitting here alone, she could enlist the help of a friend. Not just *any* friend—a friend devoted to Lucy's happiness.

Nate Mills.

She drew her phone out of her back pocket, calmed by this plan. She couldn't wait to tell him about the deleted text string—about Joanne ditching her open house to play Mom of the Year.

She scrolled through her contacts, her eyes sliding from the Ms to the Ps, then back again. There were no contacts under N at all, Nate or otherwise.

"No." Lucy scowled at her phone, then brought up the keypad to dial his number from memory. Her thumbs hovered over the numbers, frozen. She pressed her lips together, furious with herself. She couldn't recall his number from memory—not even the first few digits.

She went back to her texts with a frustrated growl,

though she already knew she wouldn't find any texts from Nate there.

When she found the unread text message at the very top of the screen, she remembered the buzzing that had jolted her from her post-sedative nap.

She squinted at the caller ID: Unknown Caller.

Beneath that: 1-11, which Lucy supposed was code for spam.

Lucy opened the text.

Just go along with it, the text read. *Do Not Resist.*

The tiny hairs on Lucy's arms stood up. It wasn't until her vision darkened that she realized she was holding her breath. She took a deep pull of air, then exhaled.

She jabbed at the phone symbol beneath the ID. Her stomach sank when she heard the tone—*beep beep beep, we're sorry, but the number you're trying to reach is no longer in service.*

Lucy pushed herself up on trembling legs. She had the sudden, wild urge to take off running again, but instead she turned and faced the house again. It looked just as desolate as it had a moment before. She wanted to think of it as an accomplice in cruel trickery, but it looked more like a victim of neglect.

She supposed she'd come here for some kind of validation—proof that the entire world hadn't undergone some total metamorphosis overnight—but she was more confused than ever.

Something drew her eyes upward, and her breath caught in her throat. She'd seen a flutter of movement in the top-floor turret window—she was sure of it.

Beyond the house, a tangle of shrubs and trees formed an overgrown barrier between the yard and the forest. A cardinal landed on the apple tree, a shock of red against the gnarled, budding branches. It flapped its wings, then let loose with a rapid-fire series of *cheeps*—the call usually reserved for announcing intruders.

She dragged an arm across her eyes, then blinked hard to clear her vision. Maybe what she'd seen in the turret window was the cardinal's reflection.

LUCY HAD ZOMBIE-WALKED FOR THREE BLOCKS, HER FEET navigating the route to Nate's house on autopilot, when a car pulled up beside her.

The driver's side window slid down, but it was a moment before she recognized her dad. The car he drove —a black Mustang waxed to a high gloss—was unfamiliar.

"There you are," he called out. He sounded worried, but his smile was enough to bring tears to Lucy's eyes. She'd never been so glad to see him in her life. "Your mom's worried about you."

Lucy fought the impulse to laugh. Her mom was worried about *her?*

"What's with the car?" She registered her dad's epaulets and white shirt, the tie off and top buttons undone. "I thought they assigned you a trip."

Her dad shrugged. "Just a quick out-and-back to JFK." He motioned to Lucy, impatient. "Jump in, kiddo. Your mom's got dinner in the oven."

Lucy took a step backward. The thought of going back home—back to The Twilight Zone—kicked her heart into a gallop.

"I was just taking a walk." She'd been going for nonchalance, but her protest sounded weak and defensive.

Her dad gave her a peculiar look. "If I return home without you, your mom will kill me. Come have dinner. Take a walk after, when you're feeling more like yourself."

Lucy crossed her arms and stared at her dad. "More like myself?"

Her dad chuckled and slid his sunglasses on. "That IV sedation is no joke." He patted the passenger seat. "Let's not keep your mom waiting any longer."

Lucy touched her back pocket and felt the comforting bulk of her cell phone. She remembered the bizarre spam text: *Just go along with it. Do Not Resist.*

She got into the passenger side slowly. "How did you know where to find me, anyway?"

"Your mom texted me your location." His tone was matter-of-fact. "You know how she gets." Lucy didn't know anything anymore—but she kept her mouth shut.

Her dad made a U-turn and headed for home.

The late afternoon sun filtered through the oak trees lining the street, but Lucy shivered as they passed the Myrtle Street house. She craned her head to see the turret, but aside from the lacy curtain drawn across it, there was nothing to see.

An involuntary grunt escaped her, but her dad didn't seem to notice.

Lucy wasn't sure of much today, but she was positive

that the curtain hadn't been closed just a couple of minutes ago.

6

———

L ucy straddled her bike, undecided.

The ride to Nate's house normally took ten minutes by bike, but she'd pedaled hard the whole way, as if she might outrun the weirdness of dinnertime if she rode fast enough.

It had been the most excruciating thirty minutes spent with her parents in a long time, the silence at the table broken by Joanne's attempts at polite small talk. On two separate occasions, she'd put her fork down to reach over and touch Lucy's forehead, the corners of her mouth turned down.

"You feeling okay, baby?"

Actually, Lucy *wasn't* feeling okay.

The spark of hope she'd felt when her dad had pulled up beside her in his car had faded. The pilot ID lanyard dangling from the rearview mirror had been familiar and reassuring, but he'd been uncharacteristically quiet and distant.

Following her dad through the front door had felt like entering an alternate dimension. Dinner looked like something out of a culinary magazine, but Lucy had only managed two bites. She'd pushed her food around her plate, summoning monosyllabic responses to her mom's questions and pretending not to notice the concerned looks her parents exchanged every few minutes.

She'd finally excused herself, claiming a need for fresh air. What she really needed was answers to the growing pile of questions taking up room in her head. She certainly wouldn't find those answers at home.

So why was she just standing here in front of Nate's house, the fireflies sending up silent flares in the yard behind her?

What was she waiting for?

It came to her in a rush—the detail that had been tugging at her all morning. Now it was as impossible to dismiss as the bizarre changes to her mom's personality, the vanished text string, and the Myrtle Street house transformation.

Nate hadn't texted or called her a single time since early this morning, before her dental appointment. He rarely went more than two hours without checking in with her during the day, but eight hours? That was unheard of.

A chorus of explanations chimed in Lucy's mind: maybe Nate was sick or in trouble, maybe his phone was broken or missing. Maybe he'd finally gotten the hint and was giving Lucy some space to breathe.

Or . . .

"Or what?" Lucy climbed off of her bike and let it clatter to the ground, disgusted by the worrywart hijacking her thoughts. "If there's anyone I can count on, it's Nate."

She strode up the front walk, aware of her pulse in her throat. The doorbell sounded inside the house, and Lucy found comfort in the familiar, low chiming.

She waited for the sound of footsteps approaching, the inevitable relief on Nate's face when he opened the door and found her standing there. She could almost imagine his breathless exclamation—*your text had me so worried!*—and imagined him folding her into his arms, his face buried in her hair.

She had already decided to let him hold on to her as long as he wanted—no eye rolls or impatient sighs from her. Not today.

The door swung open, and Lucy found herself face to face with Nate's mom, Mary. She squinted out at Lucy, who stood under the glow of the porch light. Lucy hadn't so much as glanced in a mirror since early this morning. She could only hope her appearance was holding up better than her mental state.

"Hi, Mrs. Mills." Lucy wondered if her smile betrayed her desperation. "I was just looking for Nate."

Mary cocked her head ever-so-slightly, her eyebrows drawn together in mild confusion. She smiled back, but Lucy saw the strain there.

"Nate?" Mary made no move to open the screen door. "Well, he and a friend are off planning the talent show."

Lucy stared at Mary, the wind knocked out of her.

She tried to remember a time when Nate had made plans without checking with her first, but she couldn't do it. She hadn't heard a thing about any talent show.

"I'm sorry—are you on the planning committee, too? Nate's been a little scattered lately."

"No!" Lucy hadn't meant to sound so irritated, but this latest development was the final straw. She dropped her eyes to her feet. "I mean . . . thank you."

Lucy backed down the front walk, then turned to find Mary at the screen door. She was still watching her, a mixture of confusion and worry on her face.

"Any idea when he'll be home?"

Mary shrugged. "Sorry, dear, I have no idea. This is his third meeting with her this week, so hopefully he won't be gone as late as he was last night. He's got his studies to think about."

Lucy swallowed hard, then turned on her heels and ran toward her bike. Her eyes brimmed with tears, turning the world into a twilight kaleidoscope—purple and orange and black. She lifted her bike by the handlebars, then tilted her chin to the sky. She refused to blink, to let the tears spill over, though it really didn't matter whether or not she cried—Mary had already closed the front door.

Lucy started pedaling, but the hope that had energized her on the ride over was gone, leaving her weak and woozy. She'd thought for sure Nate would be there to explain everything—a steady beacon in the darkness.

She made her way home, weaving down the street, whimpering under her breath. The exchange with Mary had confirmed her worst fears. She'd looked at Lucy as though she were a stranger—as if they'd never met before —and that set the stage for another dreadful possibility.

Maybe, when she caught up with Nate, he wouldn't know her either.

7

W hen Mr. Dillinger shuffled to a stop beside Lucy's desk, she had already filled an entire page of her notebook.

The history teacher gave her an over-the-glasses look that was easy to interpret. He'd asked the class to spend fifteen minutes copying the Civil War timeline from the board for tomorrow's test, but these weren't dates on the page. They were song lyrics—damn good ones if she was being honest.

"Your notes, Miss McGowen?"

Lucy was already flipping back a page, where she'd scrawled her timeline like a good little soldier. She gave him a smile and a thumbs-up—both acts of fraud. After the day she'd had yesterday, she had barely managed to drag herself out of bed this morning.

The thing that had kept her from staying in bed, protected from the world in her blanket burrito, was a burning need to see Nate face to face.

She needed to know for sure.

Her teacher sauntered away, satisfied, leaving Lucy to her song lyrics.

The words had come to her, a slow drip at first, escalating to a torrent she could hardly keep up with. She'd been trying with all her might to think about anything but yesterday and the alternate reality she'd found herself in, but the scribbles on the page didn't lie.

She lifted her pen from the paper as the classroom door opened. An unfamiliar girl hesitated there, the folder held in front of her chest providing weak protection against the eyes staring back at her. A cascade of dark curls draped over her hunched shoulders, a stark contrast to her blue eyes. Rosy splotches bloomed on her pale cheeks.

The teacher accepted the class-add form she offered, perused it, then gave a curt nod.

He clapped her on the shoulder. "Folks, join me in welcoming Ava. She's new to Portsmouth and to Harborview High."

Lucy scrutinized the new girl from the safety of her desk and concluded there was something guarded and sad in Ava's eyes. She tried to imagine the life event—divorce, maybe, or a family death—that would force someone to start at a new school so late in the year.

Ava stood there, stone-faced, as the class responded with a few murmurs of welcome and cleared throats. Mr. Dillinger gestured for her to find an empty seat in the classroom. There was only one, and it was beside Lucy.

Ava locked eyes with her, and Lucy lifted her hand in

a brief wave. Then the passing tone sounded, and a stampede of students scrambled from their desks and pushed past the new girl.

By the time Lucy had gathered her things, Ava was gone, swept out into the hallway with the masses.

Nate had met Lucy outside the student commons after fourth period every day for the last five months—without fail.

On some level, Lucy knew he wouldn't be there today, a smile lighting his face at the sight of her, his hand stretched out for hers before she even reached him.

She sagged against the wall that had become their unofficial meeting spot, grief-stricken and alone. She didn't realize how desperate she was for proof that this was all a giant misunderstanding—that Nate's mom somehow hadn't recognized her on their doorstep.

That there was a logical explanation for the sudden radio silence from Nate.

That he would be there waiting for her like he always was—irritatingly sweet and attentive—and she could get back to taking him for granted the way she'd taken her entire mundane existence for granted.

Then she spotted him heading for the cafeteria, his eyes on the face of the girl walking beside him. Lucy recognized the girl as Ashley Holt, who was best known for her position on the school dance team. At the last pep rally, Ashley had stolen the show with her break-away solo—which included moves that made even Lucy blush.

What wrecked her most wasn't the fact that Nate was wearing her favorite shirt—the well-worn, red plaid one he'd let her borrow just last week. It was his eager-puppy posture and the way he ducked his head so that his dark hair fell over his eyes. He did that when he was feeling nervous and shy—which is exactly how he'd felt when he'd first started hanging out with Lucy.

Only now, Ashley was the reason for his shyness.

Lucy started to turn away, to escape to a place where she could wallow in self-pity, but then something flared up inside her chest, hot and bright. It was anger—the kind that couldn't be squashed or reasoned with. It propelled her forward, across the student commons, until she was right behind Nate and Ashley.

She didn't understand any of it—this before-and-after nightmare—but she couldn't sit back and watch it unfold without a fight.

"Hey!" Lucy's voice echoed off the walls, causing heads to swivel.

There was a lull in the chaos, and Lucy felt her stomach drop. She had no idea what the next step was; she hadn't thought that far ahead.

Nate put a hand on Ashley's arm—a subconscious, protective move Lucy had seen a thousand times before, when she'd been the focus of his loyalty instead of this Barbie look-alike.

She stood there, speechless, her eyes darting between Nate and Ashley. Nate's eyebrows were arched with surprise, but Ashley wore a smirk that made Lucy bite down on the insides of her cheeks.

He's mine, so back the hell off! She didn't actually say it—she kept her teeth clenched tight—but Ashley's eyes widened as though she had. She let her gaze travel down, a split-second assessment of Lucy's T-shirt and frayed jeans.

"Oh—were you wanting to sign up?" Ashley's smile didn't reach her eyes. "We still have a couple of slots left."

Lucy dragged her eyes from Ashley's perfect teeth to Nate's face. He looked a little embarrassed. She knew his eyes as well as her own—hazel with a swirl of green and gold—but there wasn't a trace of recognition in them.

He stuck his hand out, his mouth hinting at a smile. "Nate Mills."

Lucy took his hand, her breath caught in her throat. His grip was all business, a detail that made her feel like crying.

The Nate she knew wore his emotions on the surface, for the whole world to see. He was smart, sensitive, and funny—but he was a terrible actor.

Just like that, the last of her hope withered and died.

"Lucy McGowen." Her voice wobbled then, so she didn't dare say more.

Ashley handed her a flyer from the stack she held against her form-fitting sweater. "Here's the info on the talent show, and the sign-up is on the wall over there." She pointed to the neon green poster outside the cafeteria. "Deadline is Friday, FYI, so sooner is better than later."

Lucy flicked her eyes at Nate, who was studying her face with renewed curiosity. "Have we met?" He narrowed his eyes and rubbed his chin, the way he always did when he was trying to remember something. "Chemistry, maybe?"

Lucy had been holding her breath, but now she let it seep out, little by little. He was talking about Chemistry class, but it felt like a jab from the Universe. It felt like she was meeting him for the first time again.

When their eyes connected, even briefly, she felt something she'd forgotten months ago—the undeniable charge of electricity that came with attraction.

"I had Chemistry last year," she said. She dropped her eyes to the flyer, because she thought if she looked at Nate another minute—the boy who had kissed her fewer than forty-eight hours ago but now treated her like a stranger—she would burst into tears.

Ashley started backing away toward the cafeteria, dragging Nate along with her. He went willingly, but he cast a parting glance at Lucy. There was something unreadable in his eyes—confusion or concern, maybe—but then he lifted his free hand in a timid wave and ducked his head.

"Nice to meet you," he called over his shoulder.

Lucy stood there, her heart thumping in her chest, while a formidable current of students swarmed past her as if she were invisible.

8

Lucy perched on a weathered picnic table, her ukulele cradled on her lap.

The song taking shape in her mind required her guitar—more strings gave a richer sound—but only the ukulele, a recent thrift shop score, was small enough to tuck into her backpack. It was the first time she'd ever tried to compose a song outside of her bedroom, and she felt weirdly exposed.

The scenery at Prescott Park was inspiring—flower gardens in bloom and a view of tugboats on the glassy harbor—but it didn't match the mood of Lucy's lyrics or the minor chords the song demanded.

She'd come home from school, after what had felt like the longest day of her life, to find a plate of oatmeal chocolate-chip cookies on the kitchen counter, still warm from the oven.

Joanne had written the note in careful, looping script: *Hope you had a great day! I'll be at book club until 4:30.*

Below that, her mom had drawn a heart and a smiley face.

Lucy wasn't sure which was more disturbing—the fact that her mom had baked cookies, or the thought of her taking part in a book club mid-week, which was prime time for showing homes to prospective buyers. In her recollection, Joanne had never done either of those things before today.

Lucy had found the park empty, aside from a family of ducks gliding on the water's surface. The ducks barely noticed her presence on the picnic table, but once she started strumming, the mother duck waddled ashore, ducklings in tow. The duck's mate lingered nearby, swiveling his head to patrol their surroundings, his green neck iridescent in the sunlight. A small patch of the green feathers was missing, evidence of a battle fought during mating season. He kept one eye on Lucy, even after his mate had settled down to preen in the afternoon sun, her ducklings arranged around her like a downy skirt.

Lucy lowered her ukulele and studied her feathered audience with envy. Her own family had never felt like a cohesive unit before this week, but at least they had been predictable. Over the years, they'd settled into a sort of routine: Mom immersed in work, Dad playing the peace-keeper, and Lucy safely holed up inside herself.

Everything they said and did now was a contradiction—a glitch in the routine. Even Nate was changed. He seemed to have no clue that he was her boyfriend—or that they'd ever met, for that matter.

Her song-in-progress was a litany of loss—a confession of all the emotions she couldn't share with anyone—but it felt like therapy. Holding it inside was not an option.

A grim thought occurred to her.

Maybe this was some karmic reckoning—payback for keeping Nate at arm's length all these months, for viewing his concerned texts as smothering. After the way he'd looked at her today—with the polite detachment of a stranger—she felt completely gutted. Was that how Nate felt when she ignored his texts?

Lucy picked up her phone and scrolled through her photos. Her camera roll was one of the first places she'd checked yesterday, but she had to see it again to really believe it.

Every picture she'd taken of Nate—*with* Nate—was gone. Without a trace, as if she'd never taken them.

Somehow, Lucy had managed to go two days without breaking down, but now she felt herself crumbling, her numbness giving way to panic and despair. Nothing made sense—and she didn't know who to turn to for answers.

Lucy hunched over her ukulele, whimpering, and gave in to the tears that she'd been holding back all day. She didn't stop to take a breath until she heard a single honk from the mother duck, which had stopped her feather ruffling to watch her.

Lucy blinked at the duck and swiped at her cheeks with her sleeves. Something had just occurred to her—the first concrete idea she'd had all day.

"You think so?" she asked.

The duck quacked in response, then tucked her beak under a feathered wing.

Lucy packed up her ukulele, sniffling, her mind made up. It was three miles by bike from the park, but she welcomed the endorphin dump of a brisk ride. She was ready for some answers, and she couldn't think of a better place to start than the beginning.

LUCY HAD HEARD JOANNE DESCRIBE PORTSMOUTH AS A real estate gem more times than she could count.

The town, known for its old-world charm and historic architecture, had a strict ordinance against cheap new construction, but there was one strip mall that had somehow slipped through the cracks.

Lucy would have sworn this was the place.

It *had* to be.

She'd been in a lot of pain when her dad had brought her in earlier that week, but even so, she'd taken notice of the ice cream parlor that shared a parking lot with Dr. Nelson's office. The sign that boasted Homemade Wicked-Awesome Waffle Cones had gotten her attention then, and it still hung in the window now. She'd planned to grab herself a frozen consolation prize after her procedure while she waited for her Uber ride, but then her mom had been there in the waiting room—along with her bizarre new reality.

Today, there was no sign of Dr. Nelson's office.

All of it—the smiling tooth caricature on the glass door, the tidy row of plastic chairs in the waiting room, the front desk and receptionist—gone. The only thing remaining was a sign taped on the inside of the glass window, with nothing but three numbers written in black Sharpie: 111.

She stepped off her bike, her breath coming in quick puffs, and went to the window. She wanted to see the sign better—to scan the waiting room inside to see if the glare of the sun was playing tricks on her eyes—when she saw it.

On one side of the sign, there was a single handprint, the kind made by a sweaty palm on a frosty pane. She lifted her hand and laid it on top of the print—a near match in size—without knowing why she was doing it. To her surprise, the glass was cold as ice.

The door above the ice cream parlor jingled, and a couple emerged, squinting into the sunshine. Lucy pulled her hand off the window glass, self-conscious. After the couple got into their car and drove away, she dragged her gaze back to the window—back to the place she had first woken to this nightmare.

The sign was still there, but the single handprint was already fading away.

Then, just like that, it was gone.

It wasn't until Lucy had climbed back on her bike, headed home, that she remembered the code at the top of her mystery text—the one that advised her to play along with her altered existence, like an unwilling actor doing improvisation.

The number at the top of that text was 1-11.

It was the same number on the sign at the former office of Dr. Nelson—and the address of the Myrtle Street house.

9

Lucy stood on the sidewalk in front of 111 Myrtle Street, her bike lowered to the ground.

The old house looked just as it had the day before—its charm dulled by years of neglect. There was still no sign of Joanne's big open house, or that it was for sale at all.

Out of the corner of her eye, she saw someone loping toward her on the sidewalk, a dog leash wound around each wrist. Lucy recognized the dog walker—the petite girl wearing a Harborview High hoodie, blonde ponytail swaying behind her—but her name teased just out of reach.

Then the details came rushing back to her, like metal shavings to a magnet. Her name was Ella McElroy. She lived three houses down from her, and the two of them had been best friends since kindergarten.

Memories from the past decade—sleepovers, inside jokes, fights, and make-ups—flared before her eyes like bright electrical flashes, a connection that had threatened to burn out but now hummed along as it should.

As Ella closed in, Lucy felt a pang of uncertainty. She moved her bike onto the Myrtle Street lawn and stepped aside, her eyes lowered. She braced herself for the possibility of a brush-off.

"Dude!" Ella called out.

Lucy looked up, breathless with relief. Ella referred to everyone—and sometimes inanimate objects—as *dude*, but her casual tone was undeniable.

"Are you trying to give me the old shoulder or what?"

Ella meant *cold shoulder*, obviously, but metaphor botching was her trademark. Lucy had always found the quirk exasperating, but today it made her want to weep with joy.

"Thank God," Lucy sighed. She checked the sidewalk behind her, just in case. "You're talking to me, right?"

Ella snorted and let go of one of the leashes, along with the dog that had been straining against it. The brindle boxer galloped over to dance in front of Lucy, front paws bouncing up off the pavement.

"Jesus!" Lucy held her hands up, her eyes wide. "Why'd you let it go?"

"Duh, she missed you!" Ella approached with her other leashed charge, a squat, panting corgi. "You were supposed to text me when you were feeling up to bluff."

"Up to snuff," Lucy corrected. She squatted down, and the boxer pressed her wet muzzle to Lucy's chin. "Want your leash back?"

Ella chuckled. "My leash? Please. By the way, you could've given me a heads up. She's a shameless bed hog." She put her hands on her hips and glared. "It's been two days, Luce. Would it kill you to show your dog a little love?"

Lucy blinked at Ella, stunned. She reached out to pet the wiggling boxer. The tag jingling from her collar read *Maggie*.

Her mom had mentioned something about someone named Maggie, just after her procedure.

Lucy had desperately wanted a dog before, but Joanne had always met her pleas for one with a hard no. Here, in this other life, it seemed she had one—a big one. She felt simultaneously excited and horrified by this realization. It was weird enough to witness changes in the people and places around her, but to have something brand new called into existence?

She looked into the boxer's brown eyes. "Hey, Maggie."

"If I'd known you were going to skip practice today, I would have brought her back earlier," Ella was saying. "I figured your face was blown up like a balloon and you were all drugged up or something."

Lucy crouched down again, desperate to slow her racing thoughts. Maggie lapped at her chin with unbridled enthusiasm—an act that should have made her recoil but felt familiar and soothing.

"Yeah. Practice was . . . canceled." It was a lie, of course. Lucy didn't practice anything—at least, not publicly. She lifted her eyes to study Ella's face, to wait for her friend to dole out some more clues as to what the hell she was talking about.

"You weren't at school today," Lucy ventured. "I thought maybe . . ." She couldn't share what she'd actually thought—that this version of her life was devoid of a best friend, just as it was devoid of a boyfriend.

Ella sighed and turned her attention to her own dog, which crouched on the scruffy lawn of 111 Myrtle Street. "Stayed home sick," she said. "Egads, Rosie. Same spot, every damn day." She bent to clean up after the corgi. "That isn't like Mr. Weston, canceling practice right before the show like that."

Lucy straightened up, her mind racing.

Mr. Weston was the high school choir director—the flamboyant, balding man who was notorious for his obsession with show tunes. As far as Lucy was concerned, she had never actually met him. She'd agonized about joining the choir since freshman year, but fear had always stopped her.

At least it had in her other life.

"Right," Lucy said. Her pulse throbbed in her temples.

"I don't know why I bother cleaning this up." Ella tied a knot in her bag and grimaced. "It's not like anyone lives here, but I guess right is right, whether anyone's watching, huh?"

Lucy let her eyes wander to the front entrance of 111 Myrtle Street and murmured in agreement.

"How long has it been off the market?" she asked.

She'd been going for nonchalance, but Ella gave her a funny look.

"When was it ever on the market, Luce?" Ella made her eyes big. "I can't imagine anyone buying a house with a creepy history like that."

Lucy nodded as though she was tracking. "True." All of this pretending made her wonder if she was a member of the drama club, too.

"Dude, are you okay?" Ella was studying her face, her head tilted with concern. "Your mom mentioned she's worried about you. Said you haven't been yourself the last couple of days."

Lucy smirked at that, but she felt closer to tears than laughter. "That's an understatement." She stroked Maggie's velvety ear. "I'm just tired, I guess."

Ella narrowed her eyes, then sighed. "You know you can always talk to me, Luce. About anything."

Lucy swallowed hard and nodded. "Thanks, Ella."

Her friend's offer sounded genuine, but their decade-long friendship was built on witty banter and small talk. They had an unspoken agreement: Lucy wouldn't pry into Ella's private life—or the darkness that had split her parents up—and vice versa.

"Rosie and I have to scoot on home," Ella said after a moment. "If I don't pass that test, my mom might get involved, and we both know how that goes."

Lucy made a face. Mrs. McElroy was either completely checked out or stalking Ella's teachers on social media. There was no in-between.

"Good luck," she said. "And thanks for taking care of Maggie for me."

As she watched Ella and Rosie retreat down the sidewalk toward home, her muddled thoughts circled back to the crumbs of information her friend had dropped. Lucy suspected the trail might only lead her deeper into confusion.

If what Ella had said was true, Lucy sang in the school choir and had a dog she had no actual memory of. And the house she now stood in front of—the one that Joanne secretly referred to her as her cash cow—wasn't even for sale.

The house was empty and forgotten, and—just like Lucy—it had been mysteriously reincarnated into something completely unrecognizable.

10

The Portsmouth Public Library was a brick two-story relic, built in the early eighteen-hundreds like so many of the town's landmarks.

Lucy hesitated on the front steps to check the sign on the door. The library would close up in fifteen minutes—barely enough time to begin her investigation of the history of 111 Myrtle Street.

Lucy had always thought the middle-aged woman at the front desk, Ms. Waters, looked more like an aging punk rocker than a librarian. Her hair was a spiky shock of burgundy, and today the T-shirt beneath her cardigan bore the logo *The Book Was Better*. When Lucy came in, she peered over her tiger-striped reading glasses, her light-bulb-shaped earrings jingling.

"Afternoon, Miss McGowen." Ms. Waters smiled, then went back to her book check-ins.

Lucy felt it again—the same relief she'd felt when Ella had recognized her.

"Let me know if I can help you find anything before we close up shop."

Lucy smiled at the librarian. "Thanks."

She stood in front of the computer, which had replaced the ancient card catalog cabinets that once lined the walls. She jiggled the mouse and stared at the search bar on the screen, unsure where to begin.

Lucy had expected to find an abundance of historical information on a house as ancient as 111 Myrtle Street, but her internet search had led to a dead end. She doubted she would find anything about it on the expansive shelf of nonfiction books.

She thought she might find some clues about it in an old local newspaper, but she had no idea which year—or which decade—to begin with.

Ella had implied that the house had a dark history, but how far back did that history go? A year? A century?

She kicked herself for not coming right out and asking Ella what she'd meant, but her friend was already looking at her as though she'd sprouted a third eye. Her parents could probably fill her in, but they were tip-toeing around her, too.

She was doing her best to blend in—to pretend she belonged in this alternate version of reality—but clearly, her best wasn't cutting it.

She turned on her heels and went to the check-out desk, where Ms. Waters was drumming on the desk with a pair of pencils, a blatant defiance of library decorum.

"Excuse me," Lucy said. "Where would I find the old newspapers?"

Ms. Waters pursed her burgundy lips. "We used to have microfiche."

Lucy stared at the librarian and tried to imagine what tiny fish had to do with newspapers.

Ms. Waters seemed to sense her confusion. "They used to keep condensed newspapers on thirty-five-millimeter film for better storage, but those machines went the way of the dinosaurs," she explained. "You might consider a simple Internet search if you're looking for a specific article, local or otherwise. The Portsmouth Weekly goes back a little way . . . who knows? You might get lucky."

Lucy opened her mouth to tell the librarian she'd started with that. Her search engine had yielded hits on myrtle and other shrubs, but not much else.

Instead, she nodded. "I'll try that. Thanks."

She was almost to the door when Ms. Waters called after her. "It isn't often I get two members of the McGowen family in here."

Lucy stopped in her tracks and faced the librarian. "Yeah?"

Ms. Waters stopped her counter polishing to push her glasses up. "Your mother was here with her book club just a couple of hours ago. They were like a bunch of school-girls, chattering about the author who's coming to Portsmouth on his book tour."

Lucy hoped her smile was convincing. She couldn't remember ever seeing her mom read anything besides real estate listings and magazines. "An author coming to little old Portsmouth—that doesn't happen every day, huh?"

Ms. Waters nodded. "He's touring all the sites for his stories. I've contacted the bank that owns the house here in Portsmouth to ask permission to do the book signing on the property . . . maybe even inside the house."

Lucy felt a shiver trail up her spine, though she wasn't sure why. "Really?"

The librarian nodded. "Normally I wouldn't set foot in that spooky old place—but I may have to make an exception to get an autographed copy."

Ms. Waters reached under the check-in counter and fished out a hardcover book. Lucy took a cautious step forward—just close enough to make out the book's title.

Hauntings of New England by Edgar March.

The image on the front cover was black and white, but Lucy recognized the house—the arched front door, the third-floor turret, the bird carvings.

It was 111 Myrtle Street.

THIRTY MINUTES LATER, JOANNE GREETED HER AT THE front door, a hopeful smile on her face.

"How was practice, sweets?" she asked.

"Great." She had told her parents more lies this week than she could count on both hands, but what was the alternative? Her entire existence felt like fiction.

Her mom didn't fish for details, thank God. Lucy didn't know the first thing about the choir's upcoming show, and she was afraid to dig herself into a hole by faking it.

"I'm making your favorite," Joanne sang out in a cheery falsetto that Lucy had never heard before.

In her other life, Lucy's favorite came from Portsmouth's best burger joint, but she did a quick scan of the kitchen counter: shredded mozzarella, baking pan, tomato sauce simmering on the stove.

"Lasagna?" she guessed.

Joanne beamed. "Of course." A shadow of concern crossed her face. "You look tired, honey."

She touched Lucy's forehead with the back of her hand, and Lucy resisted the urge to recoil.

"Why don't you rest until dinner? Your dad got called away on a trip, so it'll be just us girls tonight."

Lucy wasn't sleepy—numb was a better word for it—but she nodded and headed for the stairs, with Maggie following close behind.

LUCY WOKE TO A WHISKERED MUZZLE SNUFFLING HER face.

She opened her eyes to find Maggie crouched beside her on the bed, her front end lowered in a play bow.

"Hey," Lucy murmured.

Maggie snorted in response, then wiggled her back end. Lucy surprised herself by laughing.

She reached for her phone on the nightstand and checked the time: 5:30. It seemed she'd slept for an entire hour.

Lucy sighed and reached for Maggie. "What do you say we just stay here in bed until this whole thing blows over?"

The dog tilted her head, an effort to identify a word she might recognize—*treat or walk,* maybe—then whimpered.

When Lucy's cell phone dinged in her hand, she bolted upright. She had a sudden, desperate thought: maybe it was a text from Nate—proof that the last couple of days had been a vivid dream.

The text notification was still lit up on the screen. Lucy gasped when she saw the number above it: 1-11.

"No," she protested. She sank back against her pillow and swiped the message to open it. Fear bloomed inside her stomach and spread outward, leaving her hands tingling.

I never got a second chance. Don't squander yours.

Lucy sat up in bed, wide awake and breathing hard. What was *that* supposed to mean? Were these past few days a nightmare or some cosmic reset button waiting to be pushed?

And who was sending her these mysterious digital nudges?

She tossed her phone aside and pulled her pillow over her head. Maggie took it as an invitation to play hide and seek, and when she jammed her snout beneath the pillow, Lucy groaned.

She was tempted to hole up in her room, to hide from the predicament she'd found herself in, but Maggie wasn't having it. Besides, the smell of lasagna was wafting up the stairs, more proof that this new reality wasn't all in her mind.

The more time she spent here, under constant assault by details that challenged everything she knew, the more distant and dreamlike her other existence seemed.

The thought of losing her grip on that existence—of having it disappear like smoke in the wind—terrified her.

Lucy felt her stomach rumble. She freed her legs from the tangle of blankets and prepared herself for the inevitable awkwardness of dinner.

Everything around her had undergone a radical shift —her home life, her social life, her extracurricular activities—but her appetite was solid.

When Lucy entered the kitchen, Joanne was pulling the lasagna out of the oven.

She hissed through her teeth. "Ah, fudge!"

Lucy recognized the tone from her other life—it was classic, pissed-off Joanne—but the muted expletive didn't match. Joanne set the pan on the stovetop, then quietly turned the tap on to run cool water over her burned skin.

"Hoo!" Her mom clucked her tongue. "That's going to scab."

Other-Joanne would have favored an F-bomb—or a hailstorm of them—and then flung the lasagna pan onto the counter as if it were a disobedient creature deserving of punishment. She might have even reprimanded Lucy for distracting her.

But this Joanne kept her arm under the running water and glanced at Lucy.

"Would you mind pouring us something to drink,

sweets? There's a pitcher of cucumber water in the fridge."

Cucumber water? Joanne had always subsisted on coffee and soda. Lucy went to the refrigerator, then stood staring at its contents. The sad scattering of takeout containers was gone, replaced by an orderly assortment of groceries. She slid the drawers open, her mouth agape. She couldn't even identify all the fruits and vegetables inside.

"Find it?" Joanne asked. She had patted her arm dry and was setting the table.

"Yeah," Lucy said. "Is your arm okay?"

Joanne smiled and shrugged. "Of course. Mind over matter."

She brought two plates of lasagna to the table, then sighed. "I hope you're hungry. I know I am—I skipped lunch today, which is a no-no for the metabolism."

Lucy slid into her chair and picked up a carefully creased cloth napkin—a far cry from the paper towels they had always used. "Ms. Waters mentioned she saw you at book club today," she ventured.

She'd been dying to sneak a peek at her mom's copy of the book Ms. Waters had shown her at the library, but she wasn't sure how to explain her sudden interest.

Joanne looked up from her plate, her eyes wide. "Let's keep book club between you and me." She kept her voice low, though the only other soul in the house was Maggie, who had stretched out on the rug by the front door.

Lucy almost choked on her bite of lasagna. "Why?"

Joanne lowered her eyes and shrugged. "Oh, you know how your dad gets. He thinks book clubs are a waste of time—that there are more productive ways to spend the day."

Lucy made a face. "Since when does Dad care how you spend your day? Just last week he told me he wished you would take a little time off."

Joanne gave her a scathing look. "Very funny, Lucy. Your father may be the breadwinner, but I contribute a lot to this household. It's called emotional labor."

Lucy opened her mouth to protest, but then she caught herself. Her mom dabbed the corners of her eyes with her napkin. She'd clearly hit a nerve with her comment.

"I know you work every bit as hard as Dad does. It's why you're the top-ranking seller."

Joanne stared at her. "That's just mean, Lucy."

When the truth settled over her, Lucy felt a sinking in the pit of her stomach. Joanne was the glue that held their household together, but here—in this version of things—she wasn't a realtor at all.

"Mom, what I meant was—"

Joanne pushed her plate back and stood up from the table, her mouth trembling. "I don't know what's gotten into you this week, Lucy, but I've had about enough."

Lucy sat back in her chair, stunned by the irony in her mom's words. The entire world had morphed into an altered state, while she was stuck somewhere else—in her other life.

How was that her fault?

"I know your dad thinks my online real estate course is a joke—but now you?" Joanne tossed her napkin onto the table. "I'm sorry, but I need to take a few minutes."

Her mom stalked out of the kitchen, leaving Lucy alone with her confusion and shame. She'd had two goals when she'd come downstairs—to ask her mom about *Hauntings of New England*, and to get through dinner with the mom who suddenly felt like a stranger.

Somehow, she had failed at both.

11

_____

The next day, Joanne offered to take Lucy out for ice cream.

Lucy's knee-jerk reaction was suspicion. In her other life, invitations like that were rare and served one of two purposes: consolation or bribery.

"Sure," she agreed. "If you're not too busy."

The shadow crossed her mom's face before Lucy realized she'd done it again—she'd responded as if this was the old Joanne, the one who only interrupted her real estate work to warm up her coffee.

"I never say no to ice cream," she amended.

The afternoon was bright and warm. A breeze whispered through the branches of the dogwood tree that dominated their front yard, the showy white blossoms giving way to bright green leaves. Those leaves would flush a reddish-purple when the chill returned, but the thought of the seasons changing gave Lucy a pang of anxiety. What if autumn came and she found herself just as confused—just as lost—as she felt right now?

Lucy hadn't realized she'd stopped in her tracks, her eyes frozen on that dogwood, until Joanne jingled her car keys.

"You want to drive?" She stood by the car, her door open.

Her smile was natural, but it was the first time she'd ever made such an offer.

"Sure." Lucy slid into the driver's seat. She liked the idea of putting herself at the controls of something —*anything*—while her own life took a sharp turn into unfamiliar territory.

THE ICE CREAM CAME WITH A CATCH.

Lucy caught the first hint after they left the ice cream shop, each of them carrying a Homemade Wicked-Awesome Waffle Cone packed with lemon gelato. Lemon was apparently Joanne's all-time favorite flavor, though Lucy wouldn't have been able to guess it if her life depended on it.

"I'll drive from here," her mom said. "So you don't have to multi-task."

Her mom started the car, then stared through the windshield, her lips pursed, seemingly unaware of the ice cream melting onto her fingers.

"Lucy," she began. "I've laid awake for two nights trying to figure out a way to help you."

She shot her mom a sideways look. "Help me with what?"

Joanne dabbed at her hand. "Just hear me out, please."

Lucy lapped at her own cone, desperate to distract herself from the protest that threatened to bubble up and out of her. Tending to those runaway drips was oddly soothing.

A one-sided argument played in her mind: *I'm not the one who's suffered a radical self-ectomy! Unlike you—and Dad, and Nate—I'm still me!*

"I spoke with someone named Dr. Hawkins," Joanne continued. "She's not a psychologist, per se . . . but she is a life coach who specializes in teenage issues."

Lucy laughed—a sharp, high-pitched bark. "Teenage issues? Seriously?"

"You've been so angry—and so out of sorts—for weeks now."

Lucy blinked at her mom, incredulous. It had only been a matter of days since she'd crash-landed into this new life, not weeks. "Mom, that's not fair. Everything was just fine until—"

Until what?

Until you woke up as an extra in *Invasion of the Body Snatchers?*

Joanne sighed and blotted her eyes with the napkin she should have been using to combat the melting mess in her hand.

"Look, honey, I know you and your dad think I have nothing better to do with my time than worry about you, but just humor me this once, huh? One hour—and if you hate it, we'll regroup."

Lucy glared at her gelato, her mind a storm of thoughts she couldn't possibly voice. Her mom had no clue what kinds of issues she was dealing with.

"Fine," she said. "One hour."

DR. HAWKINS SAT WITH HER FEET CURLED BENEATH HER on the sofa, her shoes kicked off to reveal a pair of tie-dyed socks.

The posture was clearly meant to make Lucy feel like she was chatting with a friend in her living room instead of being paid to analyze her thoughts.

The name Hawkins made Lucy think of raptors—sharp beaks and talons designed to kill—but the doctor didn't look particularly threatening. Her face was round, her features sagging under the weight of late-middle age. Her hair was wound into a towering bun, but instead of pulling her face tighter, it added to the effect, like a dollop of icing on top of a cake.

"I thought we could take a few minutes to just chat and get to know one another," she said.

Lucy knew what that was code for: the doctor pulling bits of intel from her without revealing squat about herself.

She let her eyes wander to the wall behind Dr. Hawkins, where five prints hung, each one showcasing the moon in different phases. The print in the center—a full moon over shimmering water—bore a quote: *The Numbers Don't Lie.*

Figurines adorned the bookshelves: a chubby Buddha, a four-armed goddess, a bronze angel with spread wings.

In the corner of the room, a small table sat in the orange glow of a salt lamp. An arrangement of souvenirs plucked from nature circled the lamp—crystals, seashells, dried flowers, a bird's nest—along with a few pillar candles and a deck of cards. This was no ordinary table; it was a sort of altar.

"Tarot," the doctor said.

Lucy dragged her eyes from the altar, blushing. "Sorry?"

"The cards," Dr. Hawkins gestured to the table. "I pull cards every morning. Gives me a sense of direction and awareness."

Lucy nodded, speechless. She wondered where her mom had found this doctor's contact information. Book club? Yoga class? Was she a real doctor, or was the title an honorary designation bestowed by questionable sources— or, worse yet, assigned to herself?

"That's cool," she said. "Direction is . . . helpful."

"Indeed." Dr. Hawkins sat forward with a smile. "You can call me Abby, by the way. I have a PhD, but I find the title pretentious, don't you?"

Lucy settled into the couch and cradled a multicolored pillow on her lap. She wondered how many others had used this pillow as a makeshift shield. Abby had a spooky talent for reading her thoughts, and she felt weirdly exposed. "Abby it is."

She glanced at the clock on the wall and was stunned to find she'd only been sitting here three minutes. This promised to be the longest hour of her life.

The doctor tilted her head and blinked at Lucy. "I understand your mom's a little worried about you. Says you haven't been your usual happy-go-lucky self."

Lucy had vowed to say as little as possible—to show her mom that this was a colossal waste of time and money—but a chuckle escaped before she could stop it.

"Happy-go-lucky? Are those her words or yours?"

Abby adjusted her glasses and smiled again. "Let's start over, Lucy. Would you say you've been feeling different lately? Less like yourself?"

Lucy cocked her head and pretended to consider that. What she was really doing was taking a few beats to breathe before reacting—because she felt dangerously close to spewing profanity.

She let her fingers trace the corners of the pillow, which were dark and stiff with what Lucy guessed was a glaze of dried perspiration, tears and snot. There wasn't a box of tissues in sight.

"Would you agree with that?" Abby coaxed.

Lucy glanced at the door and leaned forward, the pillow pinned beneath her chest.

"I would say that's not even close," she said. She was ashamed of the urgency in her voice, but now that she'd started talking, there was no stopping it. "Not even in the same *galaxy* as the truth."

Abby clicked her pen, rapid-fire, while she thought that over. "Then what is the truth, Lucy?"

Lucy felt her nostrils flare with the effort of keeping her emotions in check. She hadn't realized how close she was to a total meltdown until now.

"The truth is that I'm the only thing that hasn't changed," she said. "Everyone else—my mom and dad, my so-called boyfriend—they're completely different."

Abby pursed her lips and nodded, her delight at Lucy's revelation obvious. "I see."

"Actually, there's more," Lucy continued, her voice rising. "It isn't just the people in my life that are different. It's my *entire* life—or at least major parts of it."

She longed to elaborate—to clue the doctor in about suddenly having a dog she'd never met, or singing in a choir she'd never joined, or having parents ditch their old personalities for new ones—but she was afraid of the domino effect that would trigger. She closed her mouth and sat back against the couch, her chin tucked to her chest.

Abby clasped her hands together. "It's okay, Lucy. You can tell me anything—I won't breathe a word of it outside of these walls. Doctor-patient confidentiality."

Lucy blinked back tears and shook her head. "I just want my old life back."

Abby nodded sympathetically. "The teenage years aren't easy. The key is to surround yourself with a solid support system. Do you have any close friends, Lucy? One or two people you can confide in?"

Lucy couldn't bear to look into Abby's earnest eyes, so she let her gaze drift to the whipped-cream bun on top of her head.

"Yes—no." She sighed and closed her eyes. "I really don't know anymore."

As she listened to the doctor's scribbling, a realization dawned on her, bright and clear. She could sit back and wait for the rest of her reality to unravel—passive and compliant—or she could take action to get her life back.

The numbers don't lie—but they don't exactly spell things out, do they?

"Mind if we call it a day, Abby?" She rose to her feet without waiting for an answer and headed for the door. "I just remembered I have a deadline to meet."

12

Lucy was on the verge of giving up when she found the flyer crumpled in the bottom of her backpack.

She smoothed the wrinkles out and stared at it, surprised that she hadn't imagined the entire exchange with Nate and the object of his current affections, Ashley.

Part of her was hoping she had conjured the whole thing in her mind, a byproduct of PTSD. If she'd imagined it, she could find some other way to challenge the rest of her current reality—something that didn't contradict the simple, muted life she'd lived up until now. The shadows felt so much safer than the spotlight.

Then again, maybe safety was overrated.

A quick glance at the wall clock got her moving again. The deadline for signing up for the talent show was this afternoon, which didn't give her much time to second guess her impulse.

That was good. She knew she would chicken out, given half a chance.

. . .

SHE FOUND THE SIGN-UP SHEET OUTSIDE THE CAFETERIA, the site of her last Nate encounter. Seeing him there with Ashley—and then having him look at her as though they were just meeting for the first time—had gutted her.

She'd been tempted to go back to their usual meeting spot the following day, as though a different day might bring a different outcome. Her cell phone—and a distinct lack of texts or calls from Nate—was proof enough that this was more than a vivid dream.

Her knees wobbled as she approached the sign-up sheet. In her other life, her songwriting and singing had been a well-guarded secret, a safety mechanism designed to protect her from judgment and criticism.

The Lucy in *this* reality—the version she was learning about through the eyes of other people—was already a valued member of the school choir, primed for this challenge.

So why was it so hard to reach for that Sharpie? Why did she feel like sprinting for the shadows?

"Hey." Lucy recognized Nate's voice before she turned around to find him standing there.

"Hey." She blushed as if he'd caught her vandalizing.

"We met the other day?" He grinned—the same self-conscious grin he'd given her when they'd first met months ago. He laid his hand on his chest. "I'm Nate . . . Lucy, right?"

She cleared her throat to steady her voice. "Yep. Good memory." Not as good as hers, of course. Her eyes dropped to his mouth for a split second, willing him to remember their kisses the way she remembered. She hated herself for taking those kisses for granted.

Nate glanced at the sign-up sheet behind Lucy. "Just in time, huh? What'd you sign up for?"

Lucy bit her lower lip. "Nothing yet. I was just about to."

"Cool." He jammed his hands into his pockets and ducked his head. It was obvious he had no intention of leaving.

She stood there, frozen and dumb, until he smiled again.

"I was just coming to grab the sign-up sheet, but I can wait until you're done."

Lucy considered walking away without another word. Nate could remove the sheet and go on his way, and she would be off the hook. Instead, she turned and added her name to the sheet while she imagined the heat of his gaze on the back of her head.

She wasn't surprised to see Ashley Holt's name at the top of the list. Someone had altered her last name with the Sharpie—it now read HOTT, a designation that irked Lucy more than it should have. She took a deep breath and focused on steadying her hand.

Name: Lucy McGowen.

Act: Vocal solo with guitar, song TBD.

Her writing came out spidery and nearly illegible, but it was official.

Nate held his hand out, and Lucy froze. Was this it? Had he finally come to his senses?

She blushed when she realized what the outstretched hand was for. She relinquished the Sharpie and stepped aside to let him take the sign-up sheet down.

"Hey—look at that. You and I are both doing a song for the show. I open and you close. Like musical bookends."

Lucy didn't bother to hide her shock. The Nate she knew didn't sing.

Did he?

"Look at that," she echoed.

"Maybe we should just collaborate." His smile was conspiratorial. "Join forces in a duet."

He watched her intently, as though he was considering saying more.

Lucy forced a smile, her heart racing. "That would be something."

She looked for signs of recognition—of remembering the other Lucy—in his narrowed eyes.

Instead he flashed another smile, followed by a perfunctory salute. "Catch you later?"

"Yeah," she murmured.

She stood there, reeling from their exchange, long after Nate had disappeared down the hall.

His parting words had been like a punch to the gut. Lucy wished she could catch him *earlier*—in their old, familiar life—in the relationship she'd shrugged off as insignificant.

She turned to leave, and someone across the student commons caught her eye. It was a moment before she recognized Ava, the new girl from history class. She leaned against a locker, arms folded, watching Lucy, her face unreadable.

The passing bell sounded, prompting a swarm of students to fill the commons from every direction. Lucy waited for the crowd to disperse—so long she risked being late to her next class—but Ava was nowhere to be seen.

13

L ucy headed for the school exit, her after-school plans already taking shape in her mind.

She would spend the hours before dinner at the park with her ukulele, the late afternoon sun on her face, with a family of ducks singing backup. She couldn't imagine a better distraction from the anxiety she'd been feeling all day.

Someone called out to her from down the hall.

Lucy recognized the tall girl waving at her—her pink-dyed pixie cut was unforgettable—but she couldn't seem to come up with her name.

"You coming to practice, Lucy?" When she got close enough, she nudged Lucy with her fist. "Weston was pissed that you skipped last week, though I think he secretly enjoyed having to sing your solo for you."

The girl's voice ushered in the details—slowly at first, then in a rush, the same way Ella had uploaded into her memory on Myrtle Street.

This was Bree, the good-natured soprano who normally stood beside Lucy in choir. They'd known each other since middle school. The blank space that had occupied Lucy's mind a moment ago was colored in.

"You okay, Luce?" Bree gave her a concerned look. "I can tell Weston you're sick if you need to skip again."

Lucy shook her head, blinking to clear the last of her confusion. "I'm fine," she said. "Lead the way, Breeze." She'd blurted the nickname, the last file to upload. Her face flooded with heat, but based on Bree's casual smile, she'd hit the mark.

After Bree went into the choir room, Lucy hesitated, her confidence wavering. It was one thing to fake a history with one person, but a room full of people all at once? She wasn't sure she could pull it off.

More importantly, hadn't Bree said something about a solo? That alone was reason enough to bail. She turned on her heels and nearly collided with Mr. Weston.

"Nice of you to make an appearance, Lucille," he crooned, his eyebrows arched high. "I had to fill in for you last time—which really tested my limits."

Lucy wasn't sure if he was referring to his vocal limits or his patience, and she wasn't about to ask. She faked a smile and did an about-face, her plans for escape obliterated.

She hesitated in the middle of the choir room, breathing through her nose to calm the panic blooming inside her. She moved to the space beside Bree, her legs on autopilot, while the rest of the choir shuffled into place.

Lucy skimmed the faces in the room, her heartbeat in her throat. Their names came to her, one by one, until it was hard to imagine she couldn't remember them in the first place.

She clasped her hands together to steady their shaking. Mr. Weston raised his hands to lead them in a warm-up—a charade that Lucy was prepared to lip-sync with—but then she was singing along, her voice clear and strong. Tears of relief and amazement blurred her eyes long after Mr. Weston raised his hands to signal the end of the exercise.

"Okay, gang. Let's take it from the top."

Mr. Weston sat down at the piano, and then the opening strains of a song filled the choir room. A stocky boy from the alto section moved into the center of the room toward one of the upright microphones.

Josh—his name is Josh, and he's the alto who sings the first solo.

Bree elbowed Lucy, and when she met Mr. Weston's eyes, he nodded. She realized, with sudden certainty and dread, that he expected her to move toward the other standing mic.

Lucy moved forward, then stopped short of the microphone. Josh was singing his solo part, his eyes closed with emotion.

At first, the lyrics sounded like a foreign language, but now they were as familiar as an old friend. Lucy felt her stomach relax, her panic melting into anticipation. She suddenly knew the song inside and out—every crescendo and curve—and she leaned into it with everything she had.

Lucy dimly registered the irony of the lyrics of "You Will Be Found." She'd never felt more lost than she had this week.

Tears shimmered in her eyes by the time the other choir members stepped forward to join in. She gave voice to everything that had been building up inside her for days—fear and confusion and grief—and when the last note died out, the hairs on her arms were standing up.

Mr. Weston pushed back from the piano, beaming like a proud father. He clapped, his eyes fixed on Lucy, and before long the entire choir room echoed with hoots and applause.

Lucy lowered her head, but there was no hiding the smile on her face. She knew it wasn't the first time she'd shared this part of herself—her music—with the people in this room, but their approval delivered a euphoria she'd never felt before.

She would do anything to feel that rush again, even if it meant leaving her other life behind.

Lucy was in no hurry to get home after practice.

She savored the buzz from her solo performance as she wandered along the sidewalk, the wind tossing her hair around her face.

She hardly noticed the car slowing to a crawl beside her until her mom leaned across the passenger seat, her head ducked to call through the open window.

"There you are!" There was no mistaking the worry behind Joanne's smile. "I was about to start calling the hospitals and morgues."

Lucy grimaced. "Why?" She hated to hurt her mom's feelings, but she was annoyed at the interruption.

"I must've called your phone five times in the last hour." Her mom stopped the car and patted the passenger seat. "When you didn't answer, I started to worry."

Lucy got into the car with a sigh. "My ringer was off. Besides, practice was—"

Nothing short of miraculous, she thought. *Like being born again.* "It was really loud."

"Of course." Joanne smiled and patted her knee. "Concert coming together nicely?"

Lucy nodded. "Yeah." She wondered if her mom had ever heard her sing—really and truly sing—the way she had in the choir room today. She tried to imagine this version of her mom shushing her with a scowl on her face, but she couldn't do it.

"I signed up for the end-of-year talent show," Lucy blurted. She studied her mom's face for signs of surprise —or for the distracted silence she would have gotten in her other life.

Joanne gasped with delight. "What a great way to end the school year." She shot her an inquisitive look. "Will you be singing a Lucy McGowen original?"

Lucy stared straight ahead, speechless. She'd always kept her original songs under lock and key—like musical diary entries. Putting them out there for public scrutiny would be the equivalent of walking out on stage naked.

"I'll probably do a cover," she said.

"Whatever you sing, it'll be great," Joanne said. "I know I've said it a thousand times, but I'm just so proud of you."

Lucy stared out the windshield and tried to swallow around the lump in her throat. It was the first time she'd ever heard her mom utter those words, and the shock of it was bittersweet. "Thanks."

The phone on her lap chimed with a new text notification. When Lucy saw the caller ID, anxiety flickered inside her rib cage like a jolt of electricity.

The text was from 1-11.

You will be found . . . can you help me find what I've lost?

Lucy's skin erupted with goosebumps, and they stayed there long after she darkened her phone screen.

"I've got a pot roast in the slow cooker," Joanne announced, oblivious to the rigid set of Lucy's jaw and the trembling of her hands. "Your dad's favorite."

"Mom, can you schedule another appointment with Dr. Hawkins?"

Her mom gave her a sideways look—a mix of surprise and relief. "Sure, honey. I'll call her as soon as we get home."

She was quiet the rest of the ride home, and that was just fine with Lucy. She was tired of lying to her mom—and tired of pretending that she wasn't a stranger in a foreign land, living a life that she had no memory of creating.

14

For someone who was paid to analyze the feelings of her clients, Abby wasn't skilled at hiding her own.

She looked dazed when Lucy entered her office, as though she'd just spent the last hour in deep meditation. She assumed her listening position—shoes off and feet tucked beneath her—while Lucy arranged herself on the sofa.

She reached for the pillow with the crusty corners. From behind Abby's desk, the lineup of moon prints—and the framed statement about numbers—taunted her.

"I'm a little surprised to see you again, Lucy," Abby admitted.

Lucy cringed at the memory of their last meeting and her abrupt exit. "Sorry about last time, Doctor—uh, Abby. Leaving early like that. . . it had nothing to do with you."

Abby smiled. "I try not to take things too personally."

Lucy cleared her throat. "You seem pretty open-minded."

"I like to think so."

"I was wondering . . ." Lucy twisted a corner of the cushion. This was harder than she'd expected. "The books on the shelf behind you? There's one in particular that caught my eye last time I was here."

Abby swiveled to see which book she was referring to, but Lucy was already on her feet. She went to the bookshelf, slid the book out and held it up, her heart racing. The pages were dog-eared, the cover blemished with a coffee stain. "This one here."

Abby hoisted herself to her feet with a grunt and took it from Lucy, intrigued. "Numerology—Meanings & Symbolism?"

Lucy laid a hand on her back pocket, where her cell phone was tucked. It felt warm, like a living, breathing thing—an accomplice in some sinister plan.

She nodded and sank back down onto the sofa. "You've read it?"

Abby nodded. "I consult with it from time to time . . . whenever the need arises." She flipped through the pages for a few moments, as though she'd forgotten Lucy was the one who'd asked about it—or was in the room at all. "Is a particular one showing up?"

Lucy swallowed hard. "One what?"

The doctor looked at her over her glasses, amused. "A number, dear. I'm assuming that's why you asked about the book?"

Lucy wondered if it had been a mistake, coming here

when the Internet was chock-full of information and didn't ask questions in return. "Yes, actually. More like a series of them."

Abby cradled the book to her chest, her eyes bright. Lucy exhaled, the last of her worry fading. There was no sign of concern or judgment in Abby's eyes. In fact, she was practically glowing with excitement.

"Go on, dear."

"The numbers one-one-one. Does that mean anything to you?"

The doctor's eyebrows shot up. "Angel," she whispered.

Lucy's eyes found the golden, spread-winged figurine on the shelf. "Angel?"

The doctor nodded vigorously. "One-one-one is the angel number." She flipped to the book's table of contents. "One of my favorites. Once you notice it, you start seeing it everywhere—on clocks, license plates, grocery store receipts." She glanced up at Lucy. "Have you?"

Lucy shrugged and averted her eyes. "You could say that." She slid her cell phone out of her pocket and placed it on the sofa beside her, face down. "What else do you know about it?"

Abby found the page she was looking for. "Ah. Here it is. If you're seeing these numbers frequently, it's said that angels are sending you signs and messages. The number one-one-one signifies communication, self-suffi-ciency, artistic expression, confidence . . . often the angel number one-one-one is sent to attract your attention to some personal issues you have, unresolved matters in your life that hinder the manifestation of your desires."

The doctor lifted her eyes to look at Lucy, an unspoken question on her face.

"Huh." Lucy shrugged, careful to keep her face neutral while her heart tripped over itself. "Interesting."

"Coincidences are signs you're on the right path," Abby added. "And if you're seeing this number everywhere, I'd take it as a sign that you're not walking that path alone."

A shiver trailed along Lucy's spine, and she sat straight up. It was no coincidence that she had started getting text messages from 1-11 just as she'd found herself in this weird, revised reality.

There was no denying that her music—her artistic expression and voice—had been thrust into the forefront of her existence, practically overnight.

Abby leafed through the book, murmuring to herself, lost in thought.

Lucy cleared her throat. "Would you mind if I borrow the book for a few days, Abby?"

The doctor closed the book with a clap. "Not at all. But maybe we can pick up where we left off last week. As I recall, you were feeling a little displaced."

Lucy snorted at the understatement, then regretted it. None of this was the doctor's fault.

"That's still true," she said.

She accepted the book from Abby but made no move to sit down now that she had what she'd come for. "But some things are actually better than they were before. Totally different, but better."

Abby nodded, fascinated by this revelation. "Well, that's wonderful. It sounds like you're moving in the right direction. Forward."

Lucy was still thinking about the doctor's assessment after she'd left the office and was sliding into the passenger seat of her mom's car, the numerology book tucked into her bag.

In some ways, she preferred this version of her life—the one in which her singing and songwriting was out in the open, not kept behind closed doors like a shameful deviation. She had a feeling the old Lucy would have gone on hiding that part of herself indefinitely.

This version of her life was also riddled with gaping holes. It seemed she'd traded her relationship with reliable Nate—and her freedom—for a helicopter mom. She was used to her dad being gone, but the old dad had always made an effort to connect with her when he was home. This incarnation of Jeremy felt distant and distracted, even when he was sitting with them at the dinner table.

"Good session?" Joanne asked, her voice high and pinched.

Lucy braced herself for an interrogation. "Yeah." She resisted the urge to feed her mom the information she obviously craved. "Abby isn't so bad."

"I'm so glad to hear that," Joanne said.

Lucy heard the relief in her mom's voice and sighed. She wished she was like her, so willing to accept things at face value—to pretend everything was as fine as it looked on the surface.

She couldn't ignore the fact tugging at the back of her mind, even as she was starting to grow into this new, improved Lucy McGowen. The random text messages she'd been getting weren't random at all.

They came from some other place—and they were meant for her.

15

Lucy had read somewhere that it takes thirty days to establish a new habit.

Unfortunately, she couldn't wait thirty days. She needed to retrain her brain and shed old habits—especially those that involved Nate—and she needed to do it pronto, before she made a complete ass of herself.

In the old days, Lucy would plunk herself down at the table by the cafeteria doors on autopilot, and Nate would join her there every day. There was little variation in the lunch menu, and the conversation was limited to the morning's happenings.

They'd become as comfortable as an old married couple, Nate maintaining a one-handed grip on his sandwich while his other hand rested on her thigh. She'd never thought about how impermeable and unwelcoming their two-person lunch crew must appear to everyone else —until today.

She entered the cafeteria and spotted Nate at their

designated table by the doors—only now Ashley Holt filled Lucy's spot.

Heat flared from beneath Lucy's shirt collar, and she blinked to clear her vision. She'd registered a few key details in that single glance: Nate wasn't sitting with his thigh pressed against Ashley's, and a semi-circle of chattering girls—the unofficial Ashley Holt Fan Club—flanked them on both sides. It was sickening to see them together, but at least they didn't look as cozy as Lucy and Nate once had.

She found Ella at a table near the food line, her blonde ponytail bobbing like a lifebuoy in a sea of faces. She waved Lucy over, but as she approached, she saw that Ella wasn't alone. The girl hunched beside her kept her eyes cast downward, her dark hair twisted into a braid over one shoulder. It was Ava, the new girl from history class.

"Hey." Lucy hesitated for a moment before she set her backpack down.

"Better late than whenever." Ella smiled, then widened her eyes. "Can you come with me to the vending machine for a sec? It always jams on me, but you've got that magic touch."

Ella flicked her eyes at Ava, and Lucy arched an eyebrow. "Sure, Ella. Let's go make some magic."

She followed Ella to the vending machine, and a backward glance confirmed Ava hadn't even looked up from her lunch. "What's up, weirdo?"

Ella leaned in to whisper. "Just a heads up. New girl doesn't talk."

Lucy nodded and shrugged. "She's new. I'm sure she'll loosen up——"

Ella grabbed Lucy's arm and squeezed. "No. She doesn't talk—*at all*. Like not a word."

Lucy let her eyes wander back to their lunch table and found Ava watching them, the corners of her mouth turned down.

She gave the vending machine a few raps with her fist, a panic-driven impulse, though they hadn't even fed it with coins yet.

She turned back to Ella. "You lost me, El."

Ella sighed and rolled her eyes skyward. "Ava is mute. She wrote a message to me saying so in this little notebook she carries around with her."

Lucy let her mouth drop open. "Oh."

"I just didn't want to embarrass you—or her, for that matter. Being the new girl is hard enough, right?"

"Right." Lucy knew very well how hard it was. She wasn't exactly new to Harborview High, but she was exploring all new territory. She couldn't imagine navigating it without a voice.

Ella patted her pockets and frowned. "So . . . can I borrow fifty cents?"

When they returned to their lunch table, Ava was packing her lunch bag into her backpack.

"Welcome to Harborview High," Lucy blurted. "I'm Lucy."

Ava looked up and locked eyes with her. During those brief moments in history class, Lucy hadn't registered just how blue—or how intense—her eyes were.

"You're Ava, right?" Lucy continued. She pretended not to feel Ella's elbow connecting with her ribcage. "We have History together."

Ava bent and scribbled in her notebook, then held it up. She'd written her reply in all caps: *YES, WE DO.*

She stood up and hefted her backpack while Lucy and Ella exchanged a worried look.

"Nice meeting you," Ella offered.

Lucy raised a hand to wave, as though Ava needed a visual. "See you tomorrow at lunch?" She hoped Ava saw the question for what it was: a standing invitation.

Ava gave a slight nod. She wasn't exactly smiling, but at least she wasn't shooting daggers at Lucy with her eyes anymore. She gave an exaggerated thumbs up and headed for the cafeteria doors.

Ella sighed loudly and sank down onto the bench. "That was beyond awkward," she said. "Silver cloud? I think we made a good impression."

"Silver lining," Lucy corrected, then groaned when she saw the cafeteria line. "Ten minutes until lunch is over and I haven't even gotten into the food line. I'll die of starvation by sixth period."

Ella gave her a peculiar look. "Food line? And let your mom's home-cooked deliciousness go to waste?"

Lucy hoped her smile hid her confusion. She rummaged in her backpack and found an unfamiliar insulated lunch bag inside.

"Of course, I'd be happy to trade this greasy-ass pizza for whatever oven lovin' your mom packed today."

Lucy forced a chuckle and took inventory of what her

mom had stowed in her backpack without her knowledge: arugula salad, quiche, carrot sticks and hummus, two homemade cookies. She tried to remember what she'd eaten for lunch yesterday, and the day before that, but the details dangled just out of reach.

"Dude, are those snickerdoodles?" Ella gave Lucy's spread a longing look. "Music to my mouth."

Lucy handed one over, her mind spinning. She didn't know why she was surprised to find this unlikely offering in her lunch sack—each day was full of twists and turns —but seeing it assembled before her made it all so tangible.

So *undeniable*.

Lucy's phone dinged with a text notification. She recognized the number from her other life—it was Nate's. She stared at it in disbelief until Ella cleared her throat.

"Everything okay there, Luce? You look like you've been seen by a ghost."

Lucy fanned herself with a paper napkin and let her correction go unsaid. "I'm fine."

It actually *was* like seeing a ghost—her phantom past come back to haunt her.

Lucy opened the text from Nate, her heart pounding. Was this what she'd been waiting for all week? A sign that she hadn't truly shed her old life like an ill-fitting skin?

She read the text message once—then again—before she realized she wasn't the only recipient listed at the top of the screen. It was a group text, and there wasn't an ounce of intimate subtext to be found.

Greetings, talented performers! Our Spring Talent Show is fast approaching . . . stay tuned for upcoming rehearsal dates and announcements! Thank you for signing up!

Lucy looked up from her phone, deflated. "It's about the talent show."

Ella perked up. "Did you sign up, Luce?"

Lucy nodded, then took a deep breath to lift the weight of disappointment.

"Sweet!" Ella grinned. She swiped the other snickerdoodle, but Lucy barely noticed.

On the other side of the cafeteria, Nate was gathering his things to leave. Lucy watched him, her throat tight with longing, and then it happened. He looked up and met her gaze. When he raised his hand to wiggle his fingers, her heart somersaulted in her chest.

Was he acknowledging her or someone else?

She ducked her head and turned to look behind her, where Ella was gathering her things.

Lucy had shouldered her backpack and was headed for the exit before she worked up the nerve to look in Nate's direction again, but he was already gone.

———

16

The following morning, Lucy woke up damp.

She threw her covers off and found her pajama bottoms dark and clinging to her legs. She put a shaking hand to her forehead to check for fever, but her skin felt cool to the touch.

This wasn't sweat.

"What the——?" She bolted upright, then checked the sheets beneath her. They were dry, but her auburn hair dangled over her shoulders in matted clumps. She reached up to touch the top of her head, frowning. Her hair wasn't exactly wet, but it wasn't dry, either.

A knock at the door startled her. Before she could find her voice, the door swung open. Joanne stood there, her eyebrows drawn together, a spatula in her right hand. The sight was so odd that Lucy felt the wild urge to laugh.

"Do you have any idea why the front door is unlocked?" A frown tugged at the corners of Joanne's mouth, a reminder of the stern mom Lucy had grown up with. Was the spatula meant to be threatening?

Lucy shrugged. "Sorry, no. I was the first to go to bed last night, remember?"

It was true. She had gone to bed by nine o'clock—a full two hours earlier than usual. She glanced at her bedside clock and found it was now almost ten.

"Whoa." She rubbed her eyes. "Did I just sleep thirteen hours?"

Joanne's face morphed from anger to worry. "Are you feeling okay, sweets? You do look a little pale."

Lucy stretched. "I'm fine, Mom." She'd uttered those very words more in the last week than she had in her entire life.

Joanne lowered her spatula and relaxed. She turned to leave, then poked her head back in. "Was Maggie being a pain last night?"

Lucy looked at the end of the bed, the spot her dog favored for sleeping, but it was empty. "No. Why?"

Joanne put a hand on her hip. "She was pacing outside your door this morning when I got up. I figured you gave her the boot for snoring or something. I'm surprised she didn't bust your door down to get back in. You know how she gets during thunderstorms."

"It stormed last night?"

"Lightning, thunder, the whole bit," Joanne said. "You must have been dead to the world."

"I guess so." Lucy forced a smile. Something tickled the back of her mind—a hint of a memory or a dream, she wasn't sure which.

"Waffles downstairs in five minutes, sleepyhead," her mom called over her shoulder as she went downstairs.

When Lucy swung her legs around and put them on the floor, she caught sight of her bare feet and gasped. Dried mud coated her skin up to her ankles.

"My God," she breathed.

Maggie bounded into her room, but Lucy barely noticed her sloppy, exuberant greeting. She couldn't take her eyes off of her mud-crusted toes.

Maggie put her front paws on Lucy's bed and burrowed her head beneath the covers, snuffling like a hog rooting for truffles. She emerged with something clenched between her teeth, the stub on her rear-end wiggling.

Lucy stared at her dog, her mind trying to make sense of the prize she'd unearthed.

"Drop it," she coaxed, and Maggie snorted playfully. Keep-away was one of her favorite games, second only to chasing squirrels. "Maggie!"

Lucy pried the dog's jaws apart—a skill she had no memory of acquiring—and gasped as she took the rain-dampened souvenir in her trembling hands.

It was a gull whittled out of wood—one of the weathered gate toppers at 111 Myrtle Street, its base splintered where it had broken off.

"You're okay," she whispered—though she wasn't sure if she was trying to console the dog or herself.

. . .

Lucy managed to get through a waffle and a half before she scooted her chair back.

"I was thinking about going for a quick bike ride," she said.

Her mom looked up, crestfallen. "But it's Saturday. What about our mother-daughter yoga class?"

Lucy had never heard her mom utter the word *yoga* before, and the concept of them practicing it together was unthinkable. This revelation would have blindsided the old Lucy.

"I know, Mom." She nodded. "I'll be back in plenty of time."

Joanne consulted with the wall clock, then sighed. "Okay, sweetheart. We leave the house at noon."

Ten minutes later, Lucy stopped her bike in front of the Myrtle Street house. The last of the lilac blossoms, stripped by the storm overnight, littered the sidewalk like confetti.

When Lucy squinted up at the turret window, she saw the lace curtains were parted again. She lowered her bike to the ground, then stepped over a sizable puddle to approach the front walkway.

From a birch tree behind the house, she heard the unmistakable song of a cardinal. Other than that, the street was quiet.

She hesitated as she passed through the front gate, her eyes settling on the jagged stump where the carved gull had perched, opposite its mate. In her mind's eye, she saw that bird where she'd stowed it in her dresser drawer, its spread wings frozen and useless.

She stood before the arched front door, aware that her breathing had become shallow and quick. The door was ajar, and a series of muddy splotches—bare footprints—decorated the front stoop.

She shook her head, as though someone had spoken the accusation in her own mind aloud.

Had she sleepwalked all the way here, during a thunderstorm, to break into this old house? She'd never sleepwalked before—but then, she'd experienced a lot of firsts lately.

Things she wouldn't have dreamed of doing in her other life.

What other explanation was there for her damp pajamas and muddy feet? If she hadn't broken that carved bird off of the railing and stashed it in her bedroom, who had?

Had her subconscious mind drawn her to this old house?

Worse yet, had something else?

Lucy coaxed the door open—just a few more inches —and let the breath she'd been holding hiss through her teeth. The foyer smelled faintly of mildew and rotting wood. She let her eyes trail from one corner of the octagonal room to the winding staircase that led to the second floor. The ornate banister curled up at the end, a detail meant to make visitors feel welcome, she supposed. Today, it seemed to beckon with sinister intentions.

She took a tentative step toward it, then cringed at the creaking of the floorboard beneath her feet.

"Hello?" she called. Her voice bounced off the bare floors and walls, meek and childlike. "Anybody home?"

The air was stale and heavy, and a tickle had started in her sinuses. She tried to muffle the sneeze threatening to explode out of her, but no luck. It echoed through the halls, the strings of an unseen piano in the next room reverberating like a tuning fork. She pressed her palms over her face, bracing for the next sneeze, but then she heard something behind her—another creaking floorboard.

Only she was standing still.

The sneeze died inside her, but a chill ran from the base of her spine to her skull. When the front door closed with a resounding thunk, Lucy turned to look, a scream stuck in her throat.

"Jeez!" The woman standing there looked just as spooked as Lucy. She pressed her hands to her heart and laughed breathlessly. "I was sure I was seeing a ghost."

The woman's leopard-print glasses provided Lucy with the only clue to her identity. It was Ms. Waters, the librarian, who had tied a handkerchief over her burgundy hair and wore a Violent Femmes sweatshirt and ripped jeans. She held a broom in one of her gloved hands. The sunlight streaming through a smeared window glinted off of her glasses and gave her a supernatural glow.

"Sorry, Ms. Waters," Lucy managed. "The door was open when I got here, so I came in to check on . . ."

To check on *what*, exactly?

In what world did it make sense to trespass in an abandoned house in broad daylight—or at night during a thunderstorm?

Ms. Waters flapped a hand at Lucy and grinned. "Guess we were both chasing our tails, huh?" She gave the keyring in her hand a shake, the cheerful jingle out of place in the gloomy light. "I came in to get things squared away for our upcoming author visit. . . you'd be surprised how tricky it is to tidy up without removing too much old-house ambiance. Of course, none of the lights work in this old place, so I'll have to find some antique lamps for the big day, maybe some air freshener to cover the smell of mildew."

"Potpourri," Lucy offered. "That's one of Joanne's favorite tricks of the trade."

Ms. Waters gave her a quizzical look.

Lucy shrugged. "My mom, I mean."

She looked around, dazed. There seemed to be an inch of dust on every windowsill, an elaborate network of cobwebs draped in every corner. She couldn't imagine what it had looked like before Ms. Waters' so-called tidying.

She made her way to the front door. "Sorry I barged in."

The librarian took a last look around the foyer and nodded. "No need to apologize, dear," she said. "I'm just glad it was you. When I heard you traipsing around upstairs and humming . . ." She waved a hand above her head. "Frankly, I almost peed my pants."

Lucy opened her mouth to protest but found she couldn't speak. Her pulse throbbed in her throat.

"I didn't have the guts to go upstairs, so I went out into the backyard, thinking there might be someone cutting through to the woods. I came back in, and there you were."

"There I was," Lucy murmured.

"Funny how susceptible the human brain is," Ms. Waters chuckled. "Read about ghosts, and the next thing you know, you're sure you're hearing one."

Lucy tried to laugh but only managed a strangled cough. "Right?"

"This place is remarkably well-preserved, considering," Ms. Waters made a sweeping gesture with her broom. "I've been told the original owner of the house made all these bird carvings over a hundred years ago."

Lucy swallowed hard. "That's . . . amazing."

"Darn good thing they keep this place locked up tight," Ms. Waters continued. "Keeps the riff-raff out. Vandalism may seem like a victimless crime, but a house like this feels like a member of the community, doesn't it?"

Lucy reached for the front door. "Absolutely."

When she opened the door, the sun bathed the weathered hardwood floor with light, a million dust motes swirling in the golden glow. She stepped into it, feeling like a figurine trapped in a life-sized snow globe. She couldn't wait to get on her bike and start pedaling for home.

"Thanks again, Ms. Waters." She lifted her hand in a wave, then jogged toward her bike. "Good luck."

She raised her eyes to the turret window, its darkened pane flanked by white lace curtains. Those curtains had been closed the last time Lucy had been there.

Ms. Waters had just made it clear she hadn't been upstairs. If she hadn't pushed those curtains aside, who had?

Lucy's cell phone rang—her mother, according to the caller ID.

Her mom was speaking into her ear before she ever said hello. "We're going to be late for yoga if you don't scoot home this minute," she said. "What are you doing at that ramshackle old house, anyway?"

Lucy sighed into the phone. There was something so disturbing about knowing her mom was tracking her every move.

"I just stopped for a quick water break," she snapped.

She rode home, her legs trembling from the adrenaline dump, unwilling to think about 111 Myrtle Street—about why those turret curtains were now parted, about who Ms. Waters had heard humming upstairs, and why Lucy had lied to her mom about what had drawn her to old the house that morning.

17

The following Monday, Lucy found Ava sitting at their favorite table alone, a book open in front of her.

She hesitated, then considered making a break for it. Eating her lunch alone in the media center sounded easier than trying to have a one-sided conversation with the sullen newcomer.

Last night, she'd done some internet research on what might leave a teenage girl unable to speak, but she'd hit a wall. She didn't know if Ava's refusal to speak had a physical cause, or if it was psychological. Was it an affliction or a choice?

Lucy had stumbled upon several articles about selective mutism—a disorder that can be caused by trauma, anxiety, or poor family relationships—but she didn't know the first thing about Ava or her situation.

What she did know was that Ava was likely to struggle

socially at Harborview High—unless Lucy and Ella befriended her.

Ava looked up from her book and gave a curt nod, her mouth set in a serious line. Escape was no longer an option.

"Hey." Lucy set her backpack down with a groan. "No Ella today, huh?"

Ava raised her eyebrows, a wordless response: *No shit, Sherlock.*

Lucy felt heat creeping up around her shirt collar. This was going to be harder than she'd imagined. "She misses school a few times a month—it's a chronic issue."

It was true. For years, Ella had been blaming her absences on flare-ups of irritable bowel syndrome, but Lucy wasn't about to share that with Ava. It really wasn't any of her business.

Ava scribbled in her notebook, her dark hair shrouding her face. When she held the notebook up, her eyes were cold and flat.

Lucy read the message twice, her confusion mounting. *It's chronic, but the issue isn't Ella's.*

She slid onto the bench and blinked at Ava, flustered, but the girl had turned her attention back to her book. "Okay," she said. "Care to enlighten me?"

When Ava looked up again, Lucy recoiled at the hostility in her blue-eyed gaze. She bent over her notebook, her pen scratching hard enough to tear the paper.

She held it up and sighed with obvious disgust. *It's easy to see if you take the time to look.*

Lucy let her mouth drop open and pressed a hand to her chest. "Excuse me?"

Ava was already scribbling again. Her message matched the defiant set of her jaw: *You're not the only one with struggles!!*

She tossed her notebook into her backpack, hefted it onto her shoulder, then stalked off, leaving Lucy stunned and alone. It was true; she *was* struggling—distraught about the makeover of her entire world—but she had told no one about that. Not her parents, and not even Ella.

Was it that obvious?

Lucy was gathering up her things, her own lunch forgotten, when she spotted it on the table where Ava had been sitting. It was a large brooch, a bird with outstretched wings decorated with amber-colored jewels, its neck lined with a striped collar of black and white stones. Lucy picked it up and let her thumb caress the bird's eye, which was fashioned out of a single ruby.

"European turtle dove," she said under her breath. *"Streptopelia turtur."*

She turned the brooch over in her hand and found the silver trim dull and tarnished. There was a faint inscription carved into its metal backing: *Eun Beag.*

She closed her fingers around the brooch, admiring the weight of it, then slid it into the pocket of her jeans. She felt obligated to return it to Ava in history class—but she had no intention of continuing their lunchtime conversation.

Without saying a word, Ava had made it clear that she wasn't interested in friendship, and that was fine. Lucy had lost plenty of things in the last week—her boyfriend, her independence, even the secret of her songwriting, but she still had her pride.

Ava wasn't in History.

Her seat was empty when Lucy showed up, and it stayed that way through all of fifth period. Lucy half-listened to Mr. Dillinger's musings on the Battle of Antietam, but she was still stinging from Ava's written accusations. For someone who was unable to speak—or refused to—she had said plenty.

Ava hadn't even spent a week at Harborview High, and she didn't know the first thing about Lucy or Ella. Why, then, had their exchange left Lucy so shaken?

She texted Ella before the end of class: *Hey. You good?*

Ella's response came right back: *Yep.*

Ava's silent rant nagged at her. Lucy considered pushing Ella for details on her absence, then shook the urge off. If her friend wanted to elaborate, she would do it on her own terms.

She texted again: *Can you give me Ava's number? I have something of hers.*

Ella responded within moments: *Don't have her number (sorry!)*

Lucy set her phone down as if it had given her an electrical zap. She frowned at it, then typed: *You didn't text her?*

Ella's response came back: *Nope.*

Lucy looked up to find that her class was emptying into the hallway. She hadn't even noticed the passing bell.

She sent a final text—*Feel better soon!*—then put her phone away. She went into the hall and let the ebb and flow of students carry her away, her mind still spinning with questions.

If Ella hadn't clued Ava in about why she was absent today, who had?

And did she really know anything about Lucy's struggles—or was it all just an act, the defensive strike of a displaced loner?

After school, Lucy took one look outside and knew her plans were ruined.

She had stashed her ukulele in her locker, intent on practicing her talent show song at the park, but the sky had turned an angry purple-grey. She stepped outside for a better look. The wind hissed through the poplar trees lining the school property and tossed her hair around her face. This would not be a little storm.

Lucy's phone dinged in her back pocket, and she turned to let the wind coax the hair out of her eyes.

There was a text from Joanne: *I'm stuck under a hairdryer at the salon!! Your dad is still about thirty minutes away!! Big storm coming!!*

Lucy rolled her eyes at her mom's excessive use of exclamation points, then texted back: *It's cool, Mom. I'll ride home with Bree after practice.*

Her mom replied: *Are you sure?????*

Lucy exhaled slowly, then responded: *YES!!!!!*

There was no choir practice today. But whether or not her mom knew it, Lucy had spent sixteen years fending for herself. She could open an app on her phone and get a ride home within minutes, easy. Right now, she craved some time alone—somewhere secluded—where she could push her worries below the surface and focus on her music.

Lucy ducked back into the school and smoothed her windblown hair. All she needed was a tucked-away corner, where she could find a few minutes of peace until the storm passed.

Her shoulders sagged when her phone dinged again. Had her mom bailed on her hairstylist to rescue her from certain death by lightning strike?

Lucy yanked her phone out and was seized by anxiety. The text wasn't from her mom—it was from 1-11.

Go up, where the spotlight cannot find you.

Lucy's gasp drew a concerned look from a passing teacher. She flashed him a false smile, her heart hammering inside her chest. She swept the corridor with furtive eyes—was the sender of the text watching her reaction right now?

Was she the target of a prankster?

She shuddered at the alternative—that the sender had other nefarious intentions.

An idea came to her then—one so simple she couldn't believe she hadn't thought of it right away. Maybe the message had a literal meaning.

A second-story catwalk encircled the auditorium

stage, much of it hidden in the shadows. It was a notorious hideout for stoners looking for a quick high at lunchtime, but after school it would be deserted—especially with a storm threatening.

She made her way to the auditorium, careful to avoid the eyes of passing students. The auditorium door floated shut behind her, then latched with a jarring *thunk*.

A panicked thought paraded through her mind—*what if she got locked inside the school after hours?!*—but she dismissed it. Students engaged in extracurricular activities would fill the halls until dinnertime, and she would be long gone by then.

"You could always just go straight home," she whispered to herself.

Speaking those words made her feel a little better, but they were empty. She had no intention of trading an hour of privacy for fresh-baked cookies. The auditorium was empty, and the acoustics above the stage were bound to be amazing.

The steps leading to the upper level were steep and rickety. Lucy gripped the railing, her palm sliding along the cool metal, her ukulele case in her other hand. A faint whiff of tobacco and electrical wire hung in the air.

Lucy found a spot to settle down directly behind the stage, where the slivers of light filtering through the upper curtains comforted her.

She'd brought her crumpled notebook along, but she wasn't sure there was enough light to read the lyrics. It didn't matter. She knew the song she was planning to cover in the talent show by heart: "Other Side of the

World" by one of her favorite female artists, K.T. Tunstall. The song was about distance in relationships—physical or emotional—and Lucy had never been able to sing it without tears in her eyes.

She took her ukulele out and gave it a few cautious strums. Up here, each twang was loud enough to make her cringe, but she suspected it was barely audible from the empty rows below. She played a few chords, her fingers finding them easily. She hummed the melody, her shyness lingering, while raindrops pelted the roof above her head—a staccato tapping that reminded of her popcorn popping.

She wove the lyrics in, whisper-singing the first verse, then allowing the slow crescendo to full voice. She sang it all the way through, her arms rough with goosebumps.

When she stopped singing, her breath caught in her throat. The last chord still hung in the air like fading smoke, but Lucy was focused on something else—the sound of someone climbing the metal steps.

She thought of that anonymous text—*where the spotlight cannot find you*—and felt a gnawing dread in her stomach. Whoever had sent her all those text messages was coming for her. The messenger somehow knew she didn't belong here in this reboot of reality and was here to escort her out like a spiritual bouncer.

She sat there, immobilized by fear, even after the footsteps shuffled to a stop just a few feet away, a silhouette in the shadows. A thunderclap sounded, rattling the rafters, eliciting a strangled shriek from Lucy.

"Hello?"

She recognized that voice, but she didn't trust her spooked mind. A light came on suddenly, illuminating the figure that stood just ten feet away.

It was Nate Mills.

He squinted at Lucy over the yellow glow of a battery-powered lantern, then his face crinkled into a smile. "Oh, hey. It's you."

It took Lucy a moment to remember that here—in this other life—they'd only met a couple of times.

"Lucy," she reminded him.

"Of course," he added. "Grand finale girl."

Lucy averted her eyes, grateful for the dim lighting. Her face felt like it was on fire.

Nate came closer, then sat down, cross-legged. He reached over to pull something out of a dark corner, but it wasn't until he popped the latches that Lucy realized it was a guitar case.

Since when did Nate play the guitar?

"I take it this isn't your first time up here," she ventured.

"First time this week," he said. "It's been my secret hideout for months." His grin widened. "Guess it's not a secret anymore, huh?"

Lucy moved to put her ukulele in its case, flustered. "Sorry," she said. "I only came up here because it was going to storm and—"

Nate reached a hand out and touched her arm. "Please," he said. "I was joking. I'm happy to share my hidden haven. You're much better company than the usual daddy longlegs."

He ducked his head, his eyes shrouded beneath a lock of dark hair, and Lucy felt her heart lurch. Before, she'd always found his shyness a little sad—but today it was endearing.

"You sounded great, by the way," he said, his eyes on his guitar's tuning key.

Once again, heat rolled up Lucy's neck onto her face. She hadn't felt self-conscious during her choir solo the other day, but singing in front of Nate—even in the dark —made her feel exposed.

"Thanks," she managed. Her throat was unspeakably dry. "I was really just messing around."

"I didn't recognize it. Is it a cover?" Nate lifted his eyes to look at her. The shadows cast by the lantern light gave him the appearance of a child captivated by a bedtime story.

Lucy nodded, her heart heavy. In her other life, it was one of Nate's favorite songs. "It's KT Tunstall. She's a Scottish singer-songwriter."

Nate widened his eyes. "Get the hell out."

Lucy blinked at him, speechless. She had seen that grin on Nate's face before—it was the one he saved for the most shocking revelations.

"I'm doing a cover by KT Tunstall!" he explained, his palm flat against his chest. "Still A Weirdo." His eyes crinkled at the edges. "That's the name of the song, not a confession."

Lucy was already nodding. "I know it well." Her pulse raced—a warning that she was trespassing on dangerous territory—but she ignored it. "You're a fan of KT?"

Nate shrugged. "It's the only song of hers I know." He furrowed his brows and scratched the back of his head. "Funny—I can't even remember where I first heard it."

Lucy forced herself to look away, afraid he might see the truth on her face. She had introduced him to the song herself, back when they'd first started dating.

In her other life.

Another thunderclap exploded, closer this time, making Lucy gasp.

Nate leaned in and laughed, breathless. "Guess we're stuck up here for a while, huh?"

She recognized that lopsided smile—the one that hinted at sarcasm. She was certainly in no hurry to get out of there. Did he feel the same way?

She dropped her gaze to her hands and tried to remember why she'd contemplated ending things with Nate—distancing herself from his need to know her better. It would have been easier to show him the real Lucy, but she hadn't realized that until now. She'd seen his curiosity, his vulnerability, as weakness—but it was the other way around. She'd been hiding her true self from him all those months because she was afraid.

She was the weak one.

Now here he was, sitting right here in front of her, his energy pulling her like a strong magnet.

"May I?" Nate asked suddenly.

Lucy stared at him. When he adjusted his guitar, she realized what he meant. "Sure. I'd love to hear your take on it."

Nate bent his head and played the chords, then whistled along with the opening. She bobbed her head with appreciation, but when he began singing, she folded her arms over her chest to quiet her shivering. Aside from goofing around, she'd never heard him sing before—not like this. His voice was pure and heartbreaking. She closed her eyes to hide the tears threatening to spill over.

When it was over, he lowered his head—just long enough for Lucy to swipe the runaway tear from her jawline without him noticing.

He chuckled. "It's a work in progress," he said. "I'm just glad I'll be opening. You, Lucy McGowen, would be a tough act to follow."

Lucy shook her head, mostly because she didn't trust her voice to speak yet. He knew her last name, too. Maybe he'd memorized it from the sign-up list.

Thunder rumbled in the distance, and she concentrated on breathing.

"It's weird." Nate was looking at her again, his eyes narrowed. "I'm having this total déjà vu . . . like we've been here before."

Lucy swallowed hard. "Yeah?"

He stared at her for another moment, his eyebrows drawn together, until a buzzing sound pulled his attention away.

He checked his cell phone. "Damn—I was supposed to be waiting out front ten minutes ago."

He paused to send a text message, then glanced up at her. "Time flies when you're having fun, huh?"

Lucy busied herself with her ukulele case. "I have to get going, too."

Nate hoisted himself to his feet, his guitar case strap over his shoulder. "Like I said, I'm happy to share my secret hiding spot with you—as long as you promise to not blow my cover."

Lucy nodded and crossed her heart with her finger. "You have my word."

Nate grinned and extended a hand. She made a fist—prepared for a casual bump—but he clasped her hand and gave it a squeeze before he let go.

"I hope to see you . . . before?"

Lucy stared at him, the wind knocked out of her. She'd come to think of her life in terms of *before and after* —but she'd assumed she was the only one in on it.

She took a breath to push a single word out: "Before?"

Nate smiled. "Before the talent show."

Lucy shrugged, then followed Nate and his bouncing lantern light down the steps on legs that felt like Jell-O.

She had a feeling she knew who was waiting out front for him—the amazing Ashley Holt—but it didn't matter.

Those stolen moments with Nate would stay with Lucy for the rest of the day.

18

L ucy's bare feet were numb from the cold.

She blinked hard to clear her vision, desperate to get her bearings in the darkness. She had fallen asleep in bed, but she now stood, shivering, on what felt like a sheet of ice. She stooped down, her nightshirt riding up on her thighs, to touch the ground with her free hand.

Not ice—smooth, chilled concrete.

She turned in a slow circle, her breath whistling in her throat. She realized she was clutching something cloth in her left hand, but her eyes were no help.

Where the hell *was* she? Had she sleepwalked again?

Jesus . . . was she *inside* the Myrtle Street house this time?

She pressed a hand over her mouth to hold in the cry that bubbled up inside her, then ordered herself to focus on the white shaft of light in the distance. Her panicked mind was slow to decipher what her eyes reported. The light was coming from above.

The realization struck her with an almost physical click: she was in the basement of their home.

She checked in with her other senses, desperate to back up this theory. She inhaled deeply, her nostrils flared with each breath: mildewing boxes, dusty garments, dank earth kept out by crumbling, cement walls. Low rush of air behind her—the gas water heater, hissing to life.

Her eyes slowly adjusted to the darkness filling the corners of the basement, her view brightening like a Polaroid picture.

She couldn't remember the last time she'd been down here, but it wasn't familiar. In her memory, it had provided storage for cast-off exercise equipment, victims of her dad's latest fitness whims, but now hulking shelves lined the walls.

She approached them with caution, prepared to investigate with her hands what her eyes couldn't make out. Neat rows of glass jars—the kind used for pickled vegetables—occupied the shelves. The Joanne from before didn't have time to eat a pickle, let alone preserve one. The Joanne inhabiting her current life could probably teach a class on pickling with one hand tied behind her back.

Lucy raised the cloth in her fist, then gave it a tentative sniff and winced at its musty odor. She ran her thumb over the fabric—some of it smooth, some of it rough like lace, a row of hard nubs that had to be buttons —and deduced it was a garment of some sort.

She knew there was probably a light switch somewhere down here—or at least a pull-string to turn on a bare bulb—but bolting up the stairs toward the light seemed like a better idea.

A quiet rustling in the far corner sent a jolt of adrenaline through Lucy's body, and she made her mind up. She took the stairs two at a time, her fear mounting as she approached the door. She slammed it behind her, panting. Her logical mind knew she'd been sharing the space with a harmless mouse, but she didn't stop running until she reached the safety of her bedroom.

When she switched her bedside lamp on, Maggie stretched on the bed and let out a groan—a greeting and a complaint all in one.

Lucy sat down beside her dog, then studied the garment in her lap. She kept her fists curled against her chest, as though any sudden movement might provoke it to bite. "What the hell is this?"

Beside her, Maggie resumed her snoring. The sound was enough to calm Lucy's galloping heart.

She held the garment up to study it. It was a tiny gown—too big for a doll but too small for a toddler—but it was like nothing she'd ever seen before. Time had yellowed the white fabric, but the lace trim and ornate pearl buttons were intact.

Lucy turned it over in her hands, desperate to find clues. This was the second time she'd gotten out of bed and woken up in a strange place. The broken-off wooden bird was bizarre enough, but she hadn't retrieved this dress without some effort.

Were these subconscious scavenger hunts random, or was there some deeper meaning behind them?

Lucy folded the gown carefully and set it on top of her dresser. Her limbs were suddenly heavy, her eyelids drooping. She curled up on the bed with her face inches from Maggie's whiskered muzzle, comforted by the wet sound of her wheezing.

Tomorrow, she would ask her mom about the gown—she was even willing to come clean about how she'd unearthed it—but for now, she would escape into the refuge of sleep.

WHEN LUCY WOKE THE FOLLOWING MORNING, SHE FOUND two things missing from her bedroom: Maggie—who had likely left to investigate the smell of frying bacon—and the small gown from Lucy's middle-of-the-night wandering.

She stared at the top of her dresser, where she'd left the gown before surrendering to sleep, and wondered if the whole thing had been a dream.

She made her way downstairs, then hesitated on the bottom step. Her parents were arguing in hushed voices.

"Go ahead and say it!" Joanne sounded close to tears. "You think I have too much time on my hands."

There was a pause—Lucy pictured her dad rubbing his eyes and sighing—while he gathered patience. "What I think is that you'd be a lot happier if you spent less time fretting about Lucy's every goddamned move—and my every move, for that matter!"

The sound of something clattering—a slammed cabinet or drawer—made Lucy flinch. She thought about retreating up the stairs until the fight was over, but then her mom appeared in the kitchen doorway.

Joanne held a shock of white fabric in one fist—the gown from last night.

It hadn't been a dream after all.

Lucy took a cautious step forward. "I was just about to ask you about that, Mom."

Joanne scoffed, but her eyes were red-rimmed, as though she'd been crying. "That's ironic."

Jeremy came up behind Joanne and laid a hand on her shoulder. "Why don't we take a minute to cool down—"

Joanne shook his hand off, but she kept her eyes on Lucy. "Don't tell me what to do," she hissed. "I may not be the provider in this family, but I'm her mother—full-time!"

Lucy's dad disappeared into the kitchen, and a moment later, the front door slammed.

"Mom," Lucy began. "You're obviously pissed about the dress—"

Joanne held the gown up and approached Lucy, her eyes narrowed. "This is not just any dress. It's a christening gown. A precious family heirloom from the early nineteen-hundreds!"

"Please, Mom." Lucy pressed her palms together. "Let me explain."

She watched her mom take a deep breath, then release it, her eyes closed. "I'm listening."

Lucy opened her mouth, then closed it. She wasn't sure if she should go all the way back to the beginning—

to her first sleepwalking episode on Myrtle Street—or if that would invite a shitstorm of questions she couldn't answer.

"Last night, I woke up and didn't know where I was," she began. "I guess I sleepwalked or something—but that's how I ended up in the basement in the pitch dark."

Joanne stared at her for a full thirty seconds before her face softened. She pressed her hand to her heart. "Oh, honey. That must have been really scary."

"It was." Lucy nodded, relieved to see her mom's anger giving way to concern. "I didn't even know what I was carrying until I got upstairs."

Joanne considered that, her eyebrows drawn together. "I believe you, Lucy," she finally said. "But I just don't understand."

Lucy shrugged. "I know. It makes no sense for me to start sleepwalking at the age of sixteen. I mean—why now?"

Her mom shook her head, her eyes on the gown. "No," she said. "You don't understand. This gown was tucked away in an heirloom chest in a cubby under the basement stairs." Her point-blank look raised goosebumps on Lucy's arms. "The chest belonged to your dad's parents, and he lost track of the key years ago."

Lucy swallowed hard. "Key?"

Joanne nodded grimly. "The chest has had a padlock on it since we got it. We've never been able to open it."

Lucy looked at her hands, as if she might find the explanation there.

"How did you unlock it? And what did you do with

the padlock?" There was something mingling with the pity in Joanne's eyes now, but it was a moment before Lucy recognized it.

It was fear.

"I . . . I have no idea."

It was the truth, and Joanne seemed to sense it. She stared at Lucy, then down at the heirloom gown. She nodded and wandered back into the kitchen, leaving Lucy alone with her stomach in knots.

No one had ever looked at her the way her mom just had—as though she was a perpetrator of some unnamed crime. She felt more like an innocent bystander who happened to be in the wrong place at the wrong time and couldn't remember any of it.

19

Ava wasn't at school again on Tuesday.

Lucy carried the bird brooch in her jeans pocket through an entire day until she got her fill of the pin poking her thigh, and then she wrapped it carefully in a few layers of tissue. As prickly as it was, she found the weight of it in her pocket strangely grounding.

When she got to history class on Wednesday and found Ava's seat empty again, she was almost relieved.

She had planned to hide in the media center during lunchtime for the second day in a row—pretending to not see Nate sitting with Ashley was torture after their time on the catwalk—but a quick peek through the doors changed her mind. Ella was back, sitting at their usual cafeteria table, her eyes lowered.

Lucy made her way over, careful to avoid looking at the table she had once shared with Nate.

"Hey, Ella," she said. "Thanks for saving me from another solitary lunch. Ava is as approachable as a cactus, but she's been absent, too. I was beginning to think you might never come back."

Ella met her eyes for a split second, then ducked her head and busied herself with her lunch. "Yeah, sorry to leave you high in the sky."

"High and dry," Lucy corrected. Relief edged the rest of her anxiety out. "And no biggie. I'm adaptable."

That was an epic understatement.

She considered a change of subject—the old Lucy had always tiptoed around her friend's frequent absences —but something was bugging her. She wasn't just curious to know if Ava had been telling the truth about Ella the other day. She *needed* to know.

She cleared her throat and leaned in closer. "El, is everything okay with you? I'm . . . I'm here if you need to talk . . . any time."

The corners of Ella's mouth twitched, but her eyes shimmered with tears. "I'm good."

Lucy linked arms with Ella. "You sure?"

Ella drew a shaky breath, then nodded. A single drop leaked from the corner of her eye, and she brushed it away.

"Actually, that's a total crock," she said. "I used to be able to handle things—to balance school stress with everything going on at home. But lately . . ."

Lucy felt her chest tighten.

My God—maybe Ava had been right. Maybe Ella's frequent sick days had nothing to do with irritable bowel syndrome.

"It's okay, Ella. You can tell me."

Ella's shoulders sagged, as though indecision physically weighed her down. She finally sighed and rubbed her eyes. "It's my mom."

Lucy nodded. She was afraid that if she spoke, Ella would clam up again. Mrs. McElroy was the tireless PTA president, a force to be reckoned with. She made Joanne —even the before version of her—look like a slacker.

"My God, Ella. Is she sick?"

Ella lifted her eyes, and the grief behind her gaze made Lucy flinch.

"Not physically." Ella cleared her throat. "The cheerful person you see running around, organizing and delegating and spearheading?"

Lucy nodded, her throat tight.

"That's who she is when she's feeling good. But something happens to her—completely out of the blue—and she becomes another person. It's like a storm cloud that rolls in. . . and when it comes, she can't even get out of bed to take a shower. She doesn't eat. She won't talk to me. She just . . . disappears."

Ella dabbed her eyes with the edge of her sleeve and sighed. She looked up at Lucy, blinking. "Jesus, Luce. Just telling you that—telling the truth for a change—makes me feel like I can breathe. Like I've been treading water for years."

Lucy smoothed her friend's hair back, mute with the shock of this revelation. She'd known Ella and her mother most of her life, and she'd never had the slightest clue. How was that possible?

"I had no idea, El."

"No one knows," Ella said. "It's the reason my dad left when I was little."

Lucy gasped. "Seriously? Jesus."

Ella shrugged. "He tried, Lucy, for years. Sometimes, when she's feeling good—and by good I mean, like, superhuman—she stops her meds completely. Then comes the inevitable crash. I don't blame my dad—not really. It's pretty hard to live with."

Lucy laced her fingers with her friend's. "So the IBS is just . . . BS?"

Ella's laugh was humorless. "Easier to explain physical crap than emotional crap, right? Someone needs to stay with her when it gets really bad, Lucy. I don't think I could ever forgive myself if . . ."

She lowered her head, and Lucy squeezed her hand. "I know."

It was a complete lie, of course. She couldn't imagine what it must be like for Ella—and she didn't know how Ava had sensed what Lucy had been blind to all these years.

20

When Lucy got to the choir room after school, she found the door locked and a note taped to the glass: PRACTICE CANCELED DUE TO FAMILY STUFF—KEEP THOSE VOCAL CORDS LIMBER UNTIL NEXT TIME!!

Bree, whose pink pixie cut had morphed into a deep purple since their last practice, came up beside her and read the sign aloud.

"Huh. Does singing in the shower count?" She flashed Lucy a peace sign, then left her alone with her thoughts.

Lucy wandered away, her eyes unfocused, until she realized she was standing in the auditorium doorway. Choir practice was canceled, but that didn't mean she couldn't get a few minutes of solo rehearsal in, right? Mr. Weston had practically assigned it.

The sound of the door clicking shut behind her echoed through the auditorium, and she stood still, listening. Then she took the metal stairs to the darkened catwalk two at a time.

She hadn't really expected to find anyone else up there, but she was disappointed when she wasn't greeted by the warm glow of Nate's battery-powered lantern. She considered turning around and heading right back down those steps.

The sunlit park was more suitable for practicing—and besides, if Nate showed up and found her here in his secret spot, he might think it was deliberate.

Correction: he might *know* it was deliberate.

In her other life, Lucy would have avoided such a blatant show of vulnerability at all costs. But she'd been presented with a chance to step outside her comfort zone, to reinvent herself, and she wasn't about to squander it.

Lucy folded herself into a seated position, then took her ukulele out. She plucked a chord, then smiled at the way the notes rang up here in the dark—rich and pure. She paused for a few beats, savoring it.

She began riffing, her fingers picking out an unfamiliar chord—D minor—until she was strumming effortlessly. The melody came from someplace inside her, a peculiar knowing, and she hummed it with her eyes closed.

After a few moments, she paused, her voice trailing off. A sudden waft of frosty air lifted her hair from around her neck and rustled the pages of her notebook.

She looked around, dazed. Already, the melody she'd been humming felt like a distant memory, and the last chord she'd strummed faded. She lowered her ukulele, flustered.

Her back pocket vibrated with a single buzz. She clapped a hand over her mouth and waited for the adrenaline riot in her chest to quiet.

Her phone showed a text notification from 1-11: *Hush-a-bye, baby, and sleep for now.*

Lucy read it again, then a third time, her eyes wide with wonder. Until now, the messages from 1-11 had felt like cryptic breadcrumbs. Was she supposed to know what this message meant, or was it an intercepted code intended for someone else?

What if all of it—this strange rebirth, the messages, the sleepwalking—was part of some metaphysical glitch?

She gathered her things and made her way down the catwalk stairs, the base of her spine tingling—the sensation she associated with peering down from the top floor of a skyscraper.

By the time she was standing outside, squinting in the sunshine, the song she'd been humming minutes before had ducked back into the corners of her subconscious mind, unreachable.

She pedaled away on her bike, her brain on autopilot, until she found herself in front of 111 Myrtle Street. The lawn, which had been a scruffy carpet of yarrow and white clover for weeks, was mowed in preparation for the upcoming book signing. The front walk was carefully swept, and the sweet perfume of lawn clippings hung in the air. Lucy closed her eyes and inhaled, a memory teasing the back of her mind.

She pulled her cell phone out again, as though the latest message from 1-11 might somehow make sense in the light of day.

Hush-a-bye, baby, and sleep for now.

She opened the search engine on her phone and typed the words in, verbatim, then scrolled through the results: bassinets and monitors, books on teaching babies to sleep through the night, dozens of children's stories.

A dead end.

"Seriously?" Lucy called out. She glared at the old house, as though it was to blame for what felt like an elaborate prank. "That's all you've got?!"

She held her phone up, her thumb hovering over the BLOCK NUMBER prompt, a silent threat. The moment she pressed it, her chin lifted in defiance, a wave of vertigo hit her. The world tilted to one side, the sunshine warming her bare arms flickering out.

When the horizon leveled out again, Lucy shivered in the grey light. A fine drizzle pelted her face like pinpricks, but she barely felt the sudden change in weather.

The Myrtle Street house had changed. It was now resplendent under a fresh coat of paint, the shutters straight and even, the landscaping pristine. There wasn't a single carved bird in sight. A FOR SALE sign sat to one side of the neatly edged front walk.

Lucy gasped as her view stuttered again, her head filled with a strange static buzzing. She turned in a slow circle to get her bearings.

All of Myrtle Street—the houses, the hemlock trees lining the street—was cloaked in a milky fog.

Her eyes settled on a man as he approached on the sidewalk, the fog swirling around him like water. He held a phone to his ear, his head ducked in conversation. A large dog tugged at the end of its leash.

Not just any dog—*Maggie.*

Lucy gawked at them, bewildered. Her dad, who rarely took the time to greet Maggie let alone take her for walks, seemed unfazed by the thick fog.

He didn't seem to notice Lucy, either.

"No, I totally get it," he said into the phone. "If I had a family and had to choose between time with them or poker with a bunch of smelly, middle-aged men, I'd pick my family, too."

If *he had a family?*

"Dad?" Lucy's own voice sounded tinny and flat. She knew it was him—he was ten feet away and closing in fast —but he didn't meet her gaze.

Maggie strained at her leash, her muscles tensed, her breathing labored.

Lucy stepped off the sidewalk as her dad strode past without slowing his pace. "Dude, no need to apologize. We'll catch up later."

Maggie lunged at Lucy, her dark eyes wild, her muzzle frothy with slobber. She made the sound—part howl, part whimper—usually reserved for chipmunks taunting just out of reach.

"Maggie!" Lucy called. The boxer reared up on her hind legs, a last attempt to get to Lucy, but Jeremy gave her leash a hard yank.

"Down, girl!" he snapped. "What's your deal?" He

gave another brisk tug—this one almost took Maggie off her feet—and kept walking.

Lucy watched them retreat, her mind a shocked blank, her eyes blurred with tears. After they turned the corner, she registered the sound of a phone ringing nearby. Her cell phone.

A shiver trailed from her spine to her skull.

The caller ID reported it was 1-11.

She had the wild urge to toss her ringing phone onto the lawn—to back away from it and sprint for home—but she was dizzy, and her arms and legs were dead weight.

She pressed the phone to her ear.

The voice on the line didn't wait for a greeting. The caller—

—*she, this was a she!*—

—began singing. The sound reminded her of an old-time phonograph, distant and reedy and hissing with static, the melody weightless as smoke curling from a chimney. Goosebumps erupted on her arms when she recognized it as the tune she'd been humming on the catwalk earlier.

"Child of my heart, sleep calmly and well all night and be happy . . ." The voice was faint and lilting, the vowels tinged with an accent Lucy couldn't place.

"I'm by your side praying blessings on you. Hush-a-bye, baby, and sleep for now."

The singing trailed off, leaving Lucy alone with the furious beating of her own heart. "Who the hell are you?"

The line crackled and buzzed, and Lucy teetered on her feet.

"I'm so tired," the voice whispered. The accent—Irish or Scottish, perhaps—was more pronounced now. "I canna rest until we're together again."

Lucy's view of the world flickered again—from fog to drizzle to bright sunshine in a matter of seconds—and then everything darkened around the edges and went black.

WHEN LUCY CAME TO, SHE SAT UP WITH A GROAN.

A single clover flower clung to her cheek, and she brushed it away. She looked at the Myrtle Street house, bleary-eyed and woozy. It was back to the way she'd found it earlier—dingy and vacant, but suitable enough for hosting the author of *Hauntings*. The carved birds stared back at her, indifferent.

Lucy got to her feet, feeling hung-over. She took one look at her phone and got the confirmation she needed. The most recent call was from 1-11. Her attempt to block the number had clearly failed.

The Myrtle Street house appeared normal again, at least at a glance, but Lucy had never felt less normal in her life.

21

Maggie greeted Lucy at the door with the usual exuberance, snorting and wagging her behind.

Lucy heard the familiar sound of her dad's suitcase wheels and brisk footsteps on the hardwood floor, and she froze. Moments ago, he'd looked right through her as though she were invisible, and she wasn't sure she could bear that again.

He rounded the corner and came into view before she could duck back out the front door.

"Hey," he said. He pulled his crew ID lanyard over his head and straightened it. "I'm headed out the door, but it's just a quick overnight to LaGuardia."

Lucy forced herself to smile. "Okay."

Jeremy stopped in his tracks and cocked his head. "You okay, Goose? You don't look so hot." She felt a surge of hope at the sound of her old nickname, but his eyes were already on the door behind her.

She took a deep breath and blinked away the tears that had welled up. "It's been kind of a weird day."

He gave her auburn hair a gentle tug, then patted her shoulder. "We all have off days, huh? Tomorrow will be better."

Lucy watched her dad go out the front door, his suitcase trailing behind him, just as he had done all her life. She wanted to find comfort in it—the routine she'd grown up with—but instead she felt disoriented, as though she'd found herself in a house of mirrors. She was starting to lose sight of what was real and true.

She pressed her fingers against her jeans pocket and felt the weight of the tissue-wrapped brooch, the hard angles of its jewel-studded wings. Those wings were curved in perpetual flight, but they made Lucy feel grounded and safe. She wondered if she would have found the brooch if she'd never left her other life.

What about Ava—would their paths have crossed? Did Ava even exist in the *before?*

She steadied herself on the arm of a chair when the realization struck her. Even if she could find a path back to her other life—the way things had been before—she wasn't sure she would take it.

THE FOLLOWING DAY, ELLA BEAT LUCY TO THE CAFETERIA.

As Lucy approached their table, she noted her friend's body language: straight back, relaxed eyebrows, mouth hinting at a smile. Once again, Ava was nowhere in sight.

Ella greeted her with a peace sign. "Hey," she said. "There's my lunch buddy."

Lucy grinned. Things were obviously going better for Ella this week, and that was a relief. "Yep, every day this time for as long as I can remember." That wasn't actually true, but she had adopted a fake-it-'til-you-make-it approach.

Ella grinned. "Some guy was just here asking about you." She wiggled her eyebrows. "Side note? He wasn't hideous."

Lucy felt her stomach drop. "What guy?"

Ella shrugged and dabbed her pizza with a napkin. "I didn't catch his name. He said he wanted to talk to you about the talent show—and then Hot-Pants Holt yanked his leash and off they went."

Lucy blinked at Ella. Hot-Pants Holt was the nickname they'd given Ashley in middle school before she'd truly grown into her hotness.

The guy Ella was talking about had to be Nate.

Lucy sat down at the table, her hands slowly unpacking her lunch while her thoughts spun in chaotic circles. She hadn't crossed paths with Nate since their catwalk encounter, and the thought of conversing with him in the light of day made her palms sweat.

Lucy held up her end of her conversation with Ella—a back-and-forth about the virtues of string cheese—before the urge to scan the cafeteria was too much to ignore. She adopted a look of neutral indifference, then swiveled to scan the tables behind them.

She spotted Ashley Holt, her back to them, tossing

her hair over her shoulder as she gestured to the dance team devotees on either side of her. Nate sat across from her, his chin resting in his hand. His eyes locked with Lucy's, and then he wiggled his fingers in wordless acknowledgment. He showed no signs of breaking eye contact.

Lucy pivoted to face Ella, heat rising in her face. "Sweet baby Jesus."

"What's gotten into you?" Ella raised an eyebrow, amused.

"I forgot something in my locker." Lucy tossed her lunch into her backpack. Whatever appetite she'd had was gone, and the raucous din and harsh light of the cafeteria made her feel claustrophobic.

"Good talk," Ella called after her.

Lucy made a beeline for the doors, but she didn't stop walking until she'd crossed the commons and turned the corner. She leaned against a bank of lockers, her chest heaving, acid burning the back of her throat.

She waited for the hall to tilt sideways—for this reality to flicker out like a weak signal, the way it had the other day on Myrtle Street—but nothing changed.

She was still Lucy, and she was still here, now.

"Hey!" Nate came around the corner, his dark hair falling over one eye. He sounded out of breath. "There you are."

Lucy searched for a witty response and failed. "Here I am."

Nate looked over his shoulder, then took a step closer. "Do you have a few minutes?" He jammed his hands in his pockets and gave her a sideways look, the corners of his eyes crinkling. She knew that look well—bashful and self-effacing—but it felt like a lifetime since she'd seen it.

Lucy shrugged. "Sure. It's about the talent show, right?"

Nate blushed, then dropped his eyes to study his shoes. "I mean, if I'm being honest, that was just an excuse I gave your friend back there."

Lucy blinked at him. "An excuse?"

Nate lifted his eyes to meet her gaze, and his shyness brought a wave of heat to Lucy's neck.

He shifted his feet. "The other day . . . up on the catwalk?"

Lucy pretended to sift through her memory as if this exact scene hadn't been playing in an endless loop in her mind ever since. "Yeah?"

Nate opened his mouth, then closed it. He folded his arms over his chest and looked away as if he might chicken out.

Lucy concentrated on her breathing.

The passing bell sounded, and the voices of students floated into the student commons. Lucy bit down on her lower lip, sure the chaos would cut her exchange with Nate short—a sentence of death by suspense—but it seemed to fuel him.

"This is going to sound crazy, but screw it." He stepped closer. "I feel like you and I have this weird . . . connection."

Lucy stared at him, speechless.

A shadow passed over Nate's face. "I sound like a

lunatic."

Lucy held her hands up, her eyes wide. "No, you don't." She broke out in a full-body sweat. "I mean . . . I'd be lying if I said I didn't feel it, too."

In her peripheral vision, Lucy saw Ella pass, her hands turned up, her face a mask of exaggerated curiosity. Lucy refused to acknowledge her while Nate was looking at her with such intensity.

Later, she could endure Ella's questions and agonize over whether she had imagined the longing in his hazel eyes—or whether she'd somehow conjured the whole thing in her imagination.

A smile flickered on Nate's face. "Thank God. It's nice to know I'm not losing my mind."

Lucy returned his smile. It would be nice to know her sanity wasn't slipping, too, but proof of that was hard to come by lately.

They stood there, looking at each other, until Ashley Holt sauntered up beside them. She dragged her eyes from Nate to Lucy, then tugged his sleeve.

Her glossy pout curved into a smile. "Keep me company?"

Nate let himself be tugged backwards, but not before he met Lucy's eyes again. "We can go over those details later, then?"

Lucy nodded. "Absolutely."

Nate and Ashley retreated, puppet and puppet master. Lucy waited for him to turn around—to cast another soul-searching look in her direction—but the crowd swallowed them up, leaving Lucy alone.

22

Even with her eyes closed, Lucy sensed it.

The world was undulating beneath her—a slow, rhythmic rolling that made her woozy. She shivered as a breeze whispered through her hair. When she reached to pull her blanket up beneath her chin, her fingernails dragged on something hard and damp.

She opened her eyes, a scream caught in her throat.

She wasn't in her bed—that much was obvious—but it took her a moment to realize the dancing orb her eyes had settled on was the full moon's reflection bobbing on water.

Lucy was kneeling in the bottom of a rowboat—the weathered Parks Department boat she'd seen tied at the park dock. She'd barely registered its presence where it bobbed in the shallows amid the cattails, and she never would have imagined taking it out into the harbor.

The rope that had once secured it to the dock lay

coiled on the floor of the boat, along with a rusted gardening shovel. The bottoms of her pajama legs were soaking wet, and her toes were slippery with tidal mud.

An owl hooted in the distance—five deep notes. The logical part of Lucy's brain identified the caller as a great horned owl, always the first to nest in New Hampshire after winter. The other part of Lucy's mind—the reptilian autopilot who couldn't care less about bird calls—shrieked and circled around the problem at hand.

The outgoing tide was pulling the boat toward the only thing between the harbor and the open sea—a small island which housed a crumbling, long-deserted light-house and not much else. By day, sunbathing harbor seals and shallow-hunting herons dotted the rocky shores. In the moonlight, the island looked unwelcoming—even sinister.

Lucy scrabbled for the oars, her breath whistling in her throat, but the oars were nowhere to be found. She pulled a long splinter of wood from beneath her thumbnail, tears stinging her eyes.

The park bench on the other shore—where she'd recently serenaded a family of ducks—seemed impossibly far away.

"Think!" The sound of her own voice beat back the panic that threatened to hijack her reasoning. "You've got this."

The owl sounded off again—*hoo-hoo-hoot . . . hoo-hoot*—closer this time. Lucy zeroed in on the gardening shovel between her muddy feet. She reached for it and gasped, surprised by its weight. The boat wobbled side to side, sending out moonlit ripples until she lowered herself and regained her balance.

A sudden cry rose from the rocky island behind her—a pair of raccoons scrapping, Lucy's rational mind reported—and she clapped a hand over her racing heart. She dipped the shovel in the saltwater, a death grip on its handle. She couldn't afford to lose it to the depths. That shovel was her ticket home.

She paddled, slowly but deliberately, two strokes on one side, two on the other. She peered over her shoulder every few strokes—the ancient lighthouse slowly but surely growing more distant—until her shovel finally scraped the rocky bottom of the park shore.

She climbed out of the boat on trembling legs and gathered the rope in her free hand. The rocks beneath her feet were slippery and jagged, and she lost her footing and went down hard on one knee. She didn't notice the red stain blooming on her pajama leg until she'd dragged the boat onto the shore and secured the rope around the docking post.

She lowered herself into a crouch, wincing, her hair clinging to her sweaty neck. Now that she was safely back on land, the weight of what had just happened settled over her.

If sleepwalking Lucy was capable of embarking on a two-mile barefoot hike and boating excursion, what else was she capable of?

A sound behind her—a metallic buzzing—startled her.

She turned and saw the source: a glowing rectangle lying face up in the mud.

Her cell phone.

She limped over to it. The mud released its hold on the device with a squelching sound, but the buzzing had already stopped.

Lucy checked the caller ID. There were several missed calls from 1-11—too many to count at a glance, each of them sent a minute apart.

"What the hell do you want from me?" Lucy hissed.

The phone began buzzing again. She fumbled it but recovered her grip. The caller was Joanne McGowen. As soon as Lucy answered, she could hear that her mom was crying.

"Are you okay?" Joanne croaked. "Wait, I see you— stay right there!"

Headlights swept over Lucy, and she raised a hand to shield her eyes. Logic and reptile warred inside her mind, but she already knew the only way out of this nightmare was a half-truth.

Joanne's car screeched to a stop. The driver's side door swung open, and her mom spilled out, arms outstretched. "Lucy!"

She let her mom fold her into her arms, but she retreated into the numbness that waited inside her mind. "Mom, how did you know——"

Joanne knelt in front of Lucy and smoothed her tangled hair back to study her face. Lucy couldn't bear the desperation in her mom's eyes, so she looked away.

"Maggie was scratching at our bedroom door." Her

mom's voice sounded clogged and hoarse. "I looked everywhere in the house, the basement and in the yard, before I thought to check your phone's location."

Lucy tightened her fingers around her mud-slicked phone, shivering from the night air.

A terrible thought had just occurred to her: what was stopping 1-11 from calling her again right now?

How would she explain these middle-of-the-night calls to her frantic mom, when she couldn't even explain them to herself?

She powered the phone off, hopeful that it would prove more effective than her failed call-blocking attempt.

"Can we please go home?" she pleaded.

She leaned into her mom as they picked their way over the rocks to the car. Joanne seemed grateful for the invitation to kick into mom mode, as though Lucy's limp weight against her was the validation she'd been craving.

Lucy would welcome her mom's pampering tonight— the inevitable cup of cocoa and the careful bandaging of her knee. Maybe these acts would distract her from her questions and postpone the interrogation until morning. She doubted she'd sleep another wink tonight, but she needed time to make sense of what had just happened.

What she'd been through tonight couldn't be explained as simple sleepwalking—couldn't be explained, *period*—but maybe she could come up with a way to appease her mom.

She was no longer sure whether she preferred it here in this life or in her other one, or whether she had a choice in the matter. But maybe if she had more time to figure out how those text messages were connected to these sleep episodes—and to her metamorphosis—she could find out who was behind all of it, and what they wanted with Lucy.

23

Lucy sat across from Abby, her heart trip-hammering behind the throw pillow she hugged to her chest.

She'd already endured two hours of tearful questioning from her mom this morning. Her dad was en route from Logan International, which meant she had more questions to look forward to. His interrogation would look different from Joanne's—fewer words and emotions—but Lucy feared it more than she'd dreaded getting out of bed this morning.

Abby took her time arranging her floral skirt around her folded legs and bare feet, then she peered over her glasses at her.

"Your mom tells me you had quite the adventure last night." Lucy heard the emphasis behind the word adventure—but she couldn't read the intent behind it. "She said it's the second episode of somnambulance you've experienced in the last couple of weeks."

Lucy frowned. "Som-*what?*"

"It's the clinical term for sleepwalking," the doctor explained.

Lucy squirmed under Abby's gaze, feeling as cornered as a mouse beneath a circling hawk.

"The third episode, actually," she admitted. "My mom doesn't know about the first time." She thought about the broken-off gull in her dresser drawer, its blank stare hidden beneath layers of underwear.

Abby nodded, her fuchsia-stained lips twitching with a smile. "Patient-doctor privilege," she said. "Your truth is safe here with me."

"I appreciate that," Lucy said. "It's been . . . really hard. My mom has been Googling sleep studies and childproof locks all morning."

The doctor removed her glasses and rubbed the bags beneath her eyes. "And how about you, Lucy? Do these episodes concern you?"

Lucy scoffed at that. "Well, yes. Not in the way it worries my mom—she's afraid for my physical well-being, which I get. I mean, it's pretty freaky to find yourself in a rowboat on the harbor and have no memory of getting there."

The doctor nodded. "So, what do you think, Lucy? Who do you think is calling the shots here?"

Lucy's eyes went to the four-armed goddess figurine on the shelf, then back to Abby's patient eyes. She'd been expecting a question like this, but she wasn't prepared with an answer.

She massaged the knee bandage beneath her jeans. So

much of the previous night had faded from her memory, but the pain from her gash was very real.

"My subconscious mind?" She looked for signs of disapproval on the doctor's face but found none.

Abby sat back, her head tilted to one side. "That's one possibility."

Lucy hugged the pillow tighter. "What do you mean?"

The doctor cocked an eyebrow. "I think you know, Lucy. We touched on it the last time you were here."

Lucy recoiled, alarmed by Abby's directness. Swooping in, going straight for the kill. "I'm not sure—"

"Get out of your head." The doctor's smile looked more encouraging than condescending. "Check in with your gut. Your intuition has a voice, so listen to what it has to say."

Stress had stolen her appetite for breakfast this morning, and her stomach rumbled, right on cue.

She made a face. "I think my gut has spoken."

The doctor blinked hard, a sign that she wouldn't be sidetracked by humor. "What is it saying, Lucy?"

Lucy crossed her legs, a nervous reflex, and the cushion tumbled to the floor. She didn't move to pick it up.

"We talked about numbers last time," she ventured. "It's getting harder to ignore, just like you said it would."

Abby nodded, and the whipped-cream bun on top of her head jiggled. "You're still seeing the number one-one-one cropping up?"

Lucy let her shoulders droop, her mind made up. She could play games with Abby, or she could embrace her as an ally. Both options were scary, but she was sick of pretending.

"That's putting it lightly." She nodded and took a deep breath. "Here's the truth, Abby. I've been getting actual text messages from someone with the caller ID . . . 1-11."

The memory of that phone call—the lullaby that seemed so close yet so far away—turned the skin on her arms to gooseflesh.

"Now we're getting somewhere." Abby leaned forward again, her eyes bright and alert, and Lucy allowed herself to breathe. Despite Abby's metaphysical references and New Age office décor, there was a part of Lucy that had expected her to laugh—or, worse yet, dismiss her claims. "So if these are spiritual messages you're getting—and if your sleepwalking is somehow related to those messages—we have a new set of questions to consider."

Lucy swallowed hard. "Like what?"

Abby rubbed her chin and let her eyes wander to the window. A male cardinal perched on the oak tree, its head cocked as though it was eavesdropping.

"Maybe the messenger is someone from another realm." The doctor's tone was matter-of-fact. "Someone with unfinished business."

Lucy shuddered as she considered that. Maybe the doctor was right—maybe her sleepwalking episodes weren't random. Maybe they were deliberate steps on a spiritual mission.

"I suppose." She gave Abby a pleading look. "But why me?"

The doctor shrugged. "Some people are naturally more open to receiving messages from the other side, while others have their defenses lowered by something external just long enough to be . . ."

"Targeted?" Lucy stared at the doctor.

Abby's eyes went to the window again, but the cardinal was gone. "Chosen."

Lucy thought about her tooth extraction, about the sedation that had seemingly ushered her from her previous existence to the one she now inhabited. Her physical pain was long gone, but she wasn't sure she could live with these side effects.

She sighed and closed her eyes. "I wouldn't mind being chosen if I knew what I'd been chosen to do."

Abby nodded. "For now, all you can do is keep your eyes—and your mind—wide open."

Lucy shivered as another thought occurred to her. "Abby, these so-called messages? How can I figure out who—or what—they're coming from?"

Abby bobbed her head up and down, proof that she'd been wondering the same thing. "If we're lucky, we're dealing with a benevolent entity. An angel, or a gentle spirit."

Lucy felt herself go cold all over. "And if we're unlucky?"

Abby hugged her knees to her ample torso, as if the temperature in the room had dropped ten degrees. "You seem like the lucky type, Lucy. Let's just leave it at that."

24

I n the flesh, Edgar March looked nothing like the sophisticated gentleman pictured on the back cover of *Hauntings of New England.* The author in the photo was a Vincent Price lookalike, perched in a wing-backed chair, his half-smile encircled by a salt-and-pepper goatee.

The man who greeted his readers on the front porch of 111 Myrtle Street wasn't much taller than Lucy. His sweater vest didn't quite hide his paunch, and a pair of reading glasses hung on a chain around his neck.

Lucy hesitated at the front gate with her copy of *Hauntings of New England* in her hand. She'd been prepared to come to the book signing empty-handed, but her copy had arrived on her doorstep in a padded envelope at the last minute.

She was surprised to see her mom already huddled with her book group friends on the front lawn. Ever since the rowboat incident, Joanne had practically turned her research on somnambulance into a full-time job.

She spotted Lucy and waved her over, a smile brightening her face. Lucy crossed the lawn, bracing herself for the small talk she was in no mood for.

Her cell phone buzzed with a text notification, and she hesitated.

The message was from 1-11, and it was brief: *Just play along.*

She pocketed her phone and scanned the gathering of readers on the front porch and lawn, as though the sender might be among them.

Just play along with *what?*

Joanne called out to her. "Lucy!"

She went over, a forced smile on her face. "My book arrived in the nick of time." She held it up. "But I haven't had a chance to look—"

"I was just telling the girls what you did," Joanne said, her face flushed with pride and excitement.

Lucy felt her stomach drop. "You did?"

Joanne put an arm around Lucy and beamed. "This is the first anniversary your dad has remembered in five years, and the nudge you gave him . . ." She shook her head, speechless, and gave Lucy's shoulder a squeeze.

One of the book club members, a woman with a silver bob, sighed wistfully. "It's a major win in my house when my teenager empties the dishwasher."

"She's a keeper," another woman chimed in.

Lucy's smile faltered, but she managed a chuckle. "I don't know about that . . ."

That was the truth. She had no idea what her mom was talking about.

Just play along.

Ms. Waters approached, her eyes wild behind her glasses. She looked flushed and ready to swoon, as though Elvis Presley was visiting instead of an aging nonfiction author. "Ladies, Mr. March is ready for us!"

The book club members crowded into the Myrtle Street house, chattering and giggling. Lucy wasn't surprised to find she was the youngest person in attendance—and she didn't care. She wasn't here to socialize.

She was here to get the real story on the Myrtle Street house, and to find out if there was a link between it and the predicament she had found herself in.

The Friends of the Portsmouth Library had set up a podium in the sitting room of the old house, with folding chairs arranged in a semi-circle before it for the reading. A warm breeze wafted through the open window, along with the droning of a distant lawnmower and the raucous heckling of a nearby crow.

Lucy found a seat in the back row near the spiral staircase. A shaft of sunlight streamed in through the window, illuminating the arched doorway leading into the next room. It looked like a glowing portal to another realm, and Lucy stared at it, mesmerized, until Edgar March cleared his throat.

The passage the author read from *Hauntings* was mostly a history of the Myrtle Street house itself. The home had been built in the early eighteen-hundreds as a carriage house and was renovated a century later into the three-story Victorian home it was today. The third-story turret, with its peek-a-boo view of the Piscataqua River, was added during that renovation. The house had seen very few structural changes since nineteen hundred, the same year a wealthy textile importer named Samuel Cormac purchased the home.

According to Mr. March, Cormac was an immigrant of Scottish descent, and he and his wife Cathryn had one daughter named Aoife.

The author closed his copy of *Hauntings* and peered at his audience over his reading glasses. He paused for effect —even the crow outside had fallen silent—and it felt to Lucy as though all the air had been sucked from the room.

"As the story goes, Aoife was only fourteen years old when she conceived a child of her own." Mr. March raised a dubious eyebrow. His gaze fell upon Lucy— perhaps because she was the only teenager in the room, or because she had begun twisting her hair over one shoulder, around and around, a self-soothing technique she'd adopted years ago. She squirmed in her chair and averted her eyes.

"Young Aoife was unmarried, and having a child out of wedlock was quite scandalous in those days," Mr. March said. "Samuel and Cathryn Cormac couldn't afford to have their status marred by scandal, and they were determined to keep Aoife's pregnancy a secret. After the child was born—a baby boy named Calum—keeping him a secret proved more difficult."

Someone in the audience murmured. Lucy scanned

the room and saw her mom sitting with her book club friends, her book clutched against her chest. Were those tears shining in Joanne's eyes?

"Wee Calum was reputedly a fussy baby, and his young mother soothed him by rocking him by the nursery window, located in the top-floor turret. Passersby heard her sweet lullabies all hours of the night—and rumors of young Aoife's illegitimate child began to circulate around Portsmouth."

At the mention of lullabies, Lucy's limbs twitched with an involuntary shudder.

Mr. March paused to savor the rapt stares of his audience.

"As the legend goes, tiny Calum did not survive to see the end of his first month. Some claim the infant succumbed to crib death. Others claim he was the victim of something . . . darker."

Lucy abandoned her hair twisting and wiped her palms on the knees of her jeans. She glared at the book on her lap, as though it had played an active role in the infant's demise. Beside her, Ms. Waters dabbed at the corner of her eye with a tissue.

"They say Young Aoife went mad with grief, and she perished soon after of a broken heart. To this day, there are those who claim to hear the sad, sweet lullaby of young Aoife Cormac as they pass by the old house. Locals say her father was so devastated by the untimely passing of his only daughter—the one he'd nicknamed Bird for her sweet singing voice—that he began a slow descent into madness himself. He spent his remaining days carving birds out of wood—day in and day out—and abandoned his thriving business, even his marriage. They say he whittled hundreds of wooden birds. Some of those carvings are still found throughout the Myrtle Street house, but many have been lost over the years."

Lucy stood at the end of the line behind Ms. Waters, waiting for her turn to get an autograph from Edgar March.

The truth was, she was hoping to get more than his signature.

She waited while Ms. Waters fawned over the author, her voice high and breathless with praise.

When Lucy's cell phone buzzed with a text notification, she reached into her back pocket, her heart kicking into a gallop.

It was a message from her dad: *Thanks, Goose. I think your get-away idea saved our marriage. LOL.*

There was a laughing emoji after that, but Lucy sensed her dad was only half-joking.

She texted him back: *Mom seems pretty jazzed.*

Her dad's text came back: *You sure you don't mind hanging with Ella this weekend?*

Lucy bit down on the inside of her cheek, desperate for more clues about what her dad was talking about but afraid to give herself away. Both of her parents had thanked her for something she hadn't done—consciously, anyway.

Ahead of her, Ms. Waters was running out of accolades, like a toy winding down.

Lucy shot a quick text back: *Of course not! We'll be fine!*

Her dad sent an emoji response back—a single heart—just as Ms. Waters gave up her spot in front of Edgar March.

The author grinned at Lucy, and she placed her copy of *Hauntings* in his outstretched hand.

"And who should I make this out to, young lady?" Mr. March shook his wrist, as though he'd signed a hundred copies instead of twenty.

"Lucy McGowen," she said.

The author tilted his head at that, his lips pursed. "Ah. Another Scot, eh?"

She shrugged, color rising in her face. "A little bit, I guess," she said. "On my dad's side."

Mr. March smiled, then bent to sign her book.

Lucy cleared her throat. "You mentioned a lullaby," she began. "You wouldn't happen to know the name of it?"

The author looked up and nodded. "It took me many months of research and countless interviews with locals to pin it down, actually. I would botch the Gaelic pronunciation, but you'll find the title in the Myrtle Street chapter."

Lucy blushed again. She'd all but admitted she hadn't cracked *Hauntings* open. She felt like a fraud.

"I'll have to revisit that," she said.

Mr. March winked at her, then handed her book back. "Refreshing to see a young person sacrificing their afternoon to take an interest in her town's history. Of all the haunted homes in my book, I think this one is my favorite."

Lucy felt her pulse quicken. "Why is that?"

The author stroked his goatee and shrugged. "The story behind it is just so heartbreaking. It's more tragic than scary." He sighed wistfully. "There's just nothing more potent—or more enduring—than a mother's love."

She nodded. Her mom lingered just outside the front door on the sun-dappled front porch. Their eyes met, but Lucy couldn't read the emotion on her face.

"Wouldn't you kill to know what it's like up there?" Mr. March whispered.

Lucy followed his gaze to the staircase behind them. A black velvet rope hung between the lower banisters to show that it was off limits. The rope hadn't been there a few days ago when she'd encountered Ms. Waters.

She grinned. "So I guess a tour is out of the question?"

"Too dangerous." The author winked. "They say the structural integrity of the stairs is questionable."

Lucy thought she heard a challenge behind the author's statement, but then Ms. Waters was back with her camera and more high-pitched chatter.

Out on the front porch, Joanne waved to get her attention. Lucy thanked Mr. March, then reluctantly left the table, a dozen unanswered questions bobbing in the back of her mind.

"Want to ride home with me?" Joanne asked. "I have to get a bag packed for our romantic weekend on Lake Winnipesaukee."

Finally—another clue.

"Actually, I've got my bike," Lucy said. "Meet you there?"

TEN MINUTES LATER, LUCY SAT CROSS-LEGGED BESIDE HER bike on the lawn of 111 Myrtle Street. She leafed through her copy of *Hauntings* until she found the chapter on Aoife Cormac and her tragic fate.

She looked up when Edgar March came out on the front porch, briefcase in hand.

He spotted Lucy and waved. "Next stop: Boston," he announced. "Ghost central."

"Good luck," Lucy called back.

Mr. March hesitated on the sidewalk, his head cocked.

Lucy had heard the single bird call, too—a low, harsh *kwut!*—but it was a moment before she spotted the source, a female cardinal. It perched on the turret window sill, the rosy crest on its head ruffled.

"A cardinal," the author mused. "How fitting."

Lucy raised her eyebrows at that, but she kept her gaze on the bird, which tilted its head from side to side. The bird peered into the window, enamored with its own reflection—or agitated by it.

It sounded the alarm again: *kwut!*

"Some say the cardinal is a spirit messenger," Mr. March said. "But I suppose I have a bias toward all things spiritual."

Lucy opened her mouth to respond—to tell him that this particular cardinal call was reserved for defending a fledgling from danger—but by the time she found her voice, Mr. March was already folding himself into his rental car.

She turned her attention back to the chapter on the Myrtle Street house. There it was, as promised—the title of the lullaby reported by late-night witnesses. She typed the words—*Seoithín, Seo Hó*—into the search engine on her phone. The cell signal here was spotty at best, and it was a few minutes before the translation popped up.

It was Gaelic, as Mr. March had said, but it was also familiar: *Hush-a-bye baby.*

25

When Lucy spotted Ava in the cafeteria the next day, she felt a stab of disappointment.

She reached for her pocket, where layers of tissue and denim blunted the sharp edges of the dove brooch. It was starting to feel like an old friend, and she hated to part with it.

Her disappointment gave way to curiosity. Where had Ava been all week?

The girl sat at their usual lunch table, her dark hair over one shoulder, her eyes on the notebook she was writing in.

Ava's harsh accusations—and the claims she had no business making—were in the forefront of Lucy's mind, but she resolved to approach with a smile. She wanted to return the brooch to its rightful owner, but she would rather do it without making a scene.

When Lucy set her things down on the table, Ava

looked up, her eyes red-rimmed and glossy. In that moment, Lucy's façade—polite detachment—melted away.

"Hey, Ava," she said. "Is everything okay?"

Ava swiped at her cheek and shrugged. She held up the notebook, where she'd already scribbled a response. *It will be soon enough.*

Lucy sat down and spread her things out, an effort to buy time. How was she supposed to respond to that—acknowledge, pursue, or ignore?

Without Ella here to balance them out and provide comic relief, this lunch period was doomed.

"Ella usually beats me here." She scanned the cafeteria, careful to avoid the Ashley-Nate zone. She hadn't seen Nate since their awkward hallway confession, but she had replayed their conversation in her mind every night since. "I saw her after first period this morning. She must have gone home early."

Ava leveled her with a deadpan look, then wrote a response in her notebook: *You think?*

Lucy sighed, her mind made up. She didn't owe Ava a thing, and she was in no mood to be the target of her unspoken jabs.

This called for a new plan: retreat!

She glanced at her phone and made a face. "Oh, jeez. I have to go."

Ava lifted her eyes and gave a slight nod.

Lucy had hoisted her backpack onto her shoulder before she remembered the brooch in her pocket. She carefully fished it out and unwrapped it, aware that Ava was watching her out of the corner of her eye.

"I believe you left this behind the other day," she said. She held it out in her outstretched hand, smiling to hide her reluctance. "I thought about turning it in to the school lost and found, but I couldn't stand the thought of it mingling with the sweaty jockstraps and water bottles."

Ava reached for the brooch, her lips parted in surprise. She met Lucy's cautious gaze, then smiled.

It was more of a thank-you than Lucy had expected. She shifted her weight, her courage boosted by the sudden change in Ava's mood. "It looks old . . . and valuable."

Ava inspected the brooch and blinked back tears. She scribbled one word in all caps: *VERY.*

A strained silence fell between them.

Lucy hesitated, her curiosity piqued. "The other day," she ventured. "How did you know—about Ella? Did she confide in you?"

Ava flipped her dark hair over her shoulder. She brought her pen to her notebook, her jaw clenched as she wrote. She held it up, her eyes averted, but her written response—three big question marks—made Lucy frown.

She blinked at Ava. "You hinted at the real reason Ella stays home sick so much—and implied that I was a dumbass for not knowing the truth, remember?"

Ava shrugged, but she didn't reach for her pen. She tucked the brooch into a backpack pocket—slowly, deliberately—then zipped it shut. Then she stood up, her blue eyes smoldering with an unspoken challenge.

She turned to stalk off, and Lucy stood there, smarting. "You don't even know Ella—or me. And, by the way, we're both doing just fine!"

Ava tossed a look over her shoulder, just long enough for Lucy to see her smirk—proof that she could see through Lucy's lie. She *wasn't* fine—not even in the same galaxy as fine.

She hated the idea that Ava, this virtual stranger, seemed to know that. She couldn't bear the thought that Ella wasn't fine either—and that all these years, she'd been too self-absorbed to see it.

Lucy stopped by Ella's house after school.

The curtains were drawn across the front windows, and the morning newspaper still lay on the front doorstep where it had landed.

She hesitated, her finger poised by the doorbell. Ella was likely tending to the mom who usually took care of everyone and everything. If she was in her best friend's shoes, would she want a visitor?

Probably not.

She was turning to leave when the front door opened. Ella popped her head out, her blonde hair in a disheveled ponytail, her T-shirt marred with a mystery stain.

"Oh, hey," she said. She stepped out onto the stoop and closed the door behind her softly. "It's you."

Lucy pretended to be offended. "Try not to look so excited to see me."

Ella leaned against the door frame, and that's when Lucy saw the exhaustion in her friend's eyes.

"I was expecting the pizza guy," she said. "I don't think the kitchen can handle another one of my so-called meals."

Lucy nodded, and they both fell silent for a couple of moments.

"How's your mom?" she asked.

Ella shrugged, but her frown was telling. "Not awesome."

"Anything I can do to help?"

Ella shook her head and met her eyes. "Just knowing you're down the street helps, Luce."

Lucy had planned to ask her friend if she could crash at her house, or vice versa, while her parents were off at Lake Winnipesaukee. Clearly, Ella's weekend would be occupied by things more pressing than gossip, nail polish, and B-grade movies. She was in survival mode.

A car pulled up at the curb—pizza guy to the rescue—and Lucy reached out to give Ella's arm a squeeze.

"Remember to take care of you, too, okay?"

LUCY HEADED HOME, LOST IN THOUGHT ABOUT ELLA AND her mom—and about her own mom and dad, who seemed as foreign to her as this strange new life.

Once she got home, she would pretend to make preparations for her weekend with Ella while her parents packed for their anniversary get-away. She relished the thought of having the weekend to herself, but the prospect of spending two nights completely alone, with only a snoring boxer for company, worried her.

What choice did she have? Ella had her hands full with her mom, and Lucy was on her own.

26

When Lucy came to, her teeth were chattering.

Just enough moonlight filtered through the trees for her to confirm that the spongy surface she was kneeling on wasn't her bed—it was moss-covered earth.

Outside again.

Something tickled her bare arm, and she gave it a violent shake. A harmless spider, most likely, but panic had turned all of Lucy's senses up high.

The sweatpants and T-shirt she'd fallen asleep in were slightly damp—especially her mud-smeared knees—but there was no sign that she'd been in the harbor.

Despite the chilly night air, her skin was bathed in sweat. Her arms trembled from a burst of exertion she had no memory of.

She turned to scan her surroundings, and her shoulder brushed a rain-soaked fern, wetting her tangled hair. She certainly wasn't on the shores of the Piscataqua, based on the trees surrounding her.

So where the hell was she?

A branch snapped nearby, causing a sudden tightening in Lucy's stomach.

"Maggie?" It was more of a whisper than a call, but she felt ridiculous for it. Yes, her dog had been curled up beside her in bed when she'd dozed off, her paws twitching with whatever doggie dream she was having, but that was no reason to think Maggie was here with her now.

Where exactly was *here*?

Lucy froze, her heart hammering in her chest, listening.

A breeze hissed through the trees and teased her hair from her neck. Something launched from the branches of a nearby tree, wings beating the air, then let out a long, piercing screech that made her clap her hand over her chest. Lucy matched the distinct cry with the pale, heart-shaped face in her mind's eye—a male barn owl, probably inviting a female to nest. The harsh shriek came again, farther away, and then Lucy was left with nothing but the sound of her own shallow breathing.

She crouched, then slowly stood, cringing at the wet crunch of pine needles and God-knows-what-else beneath her bare feet. A sudden buzzing on her thigh made her cry out. The pocket of her sweatpants was lit from the inside, the rectangle shape of her cell phone visible through the fabric.

She drew it out with dirt-caked fingers and saw the text notification. She was almost relieved to see it was from 1-11, as if the sender was an anonymous friend and not some spiritual stalker.

The message was short and to the point: *Bring him home.*

Lucy looked around, dazed, as though some unseen nocturnal critter might offer insight.

As if she wasn't in this nightmare completely alone.

"Perfect," she breathed.

A pair of headlights cut through the darkness and swept over the trees on both sides of Lucy, just long enough for her to establish that she was on a narrow trail, not more than two hundred yards from where the car idled.

Lucy held her breath and waited. A car door opened, then slammed, and a smaller light danced through the forest, coming closer.

She felt paralyzed, torn between hope and fear.

Had her mom checked her cell phone location and demanded she and her dad drive the hour from Lake Winnipesaukee to rescue her? Would they decide Lucy's sleepwalking warranted something more drastic than a home alarm system?

How would she explain her presence here if she didn't understand it herself?

A new possibility occurred to her: maybe the glow bouncing toward her wasn't her parents on a middle-of-the-night rescue mission.

Maybe the source was malevolent.

Maybe—Lucy pressed a hand over her mouth to stifle

a whimper—maybe whatever was coming her way meant to do her harm.

When the light found her, she squinted at it, her body folded into a defensive crouch.

"Lucy?" The voice was familiar, but it didn't belong to her mom or dad.

She exhaled, her breath a white puff in the glow of that disembodied light. "Who's there?"

The light turned, illuminating a torso before it jerked upward and turned the face into a grotesque mask of angles and shadows.

"It's me," the voice said. "Nate Mills?"

Lucy reached a hand out to steady herself on the moss-covered boulder beside her.

"Nate?" She tried to stand up, but the adrenaline dump had left her legs weak. "What are you doing here?"

The question sounded ridiculous, considering her current position.

Nate brandished his phone and sputtered. "You sent me your location—like, three times. I tried to call you, but the calls wouldn't go through."

"I did?"

Nate consulted his phone, his face glowing in the screen's light. His eyebrows were furrowed, but he looked more worried than irritated, and Lucy felt herself relax.

"Yep," he said. "Shows it right here—sent exactly one minute apart."

Lucy reached for her own cell phone, then thought better of it. Clearly, Nate was telling her the truth. How else could she explain him showing up out here—now?

She attempted to stand up again, and this time her legs cooperated. "Do you think you could give me a ride home?"

"Of course," Nate said. He took two steps toward her, then halted, his cell phone glare frozen on Lucy's legs. "Whoa."

Lucy bent to look at the focus of Nate's attention—her knees were even muddier than she'd realized—but he wasn't looking at her legs. He stooped to get a closer look at the boulder beside her. The light of his cell phone wobbled on the stone—proof that he was as shaky as she was.

This was no ordinary stone.

It was a rudimentary headstone, or at least part of one. The lower half of it was only partially excavated, the dark earth scooped and clawed away.

Lucy brought her hands to her face—her fingernails were packed with wet soil—and gasped. "Jesus."

"Is that a grave?" Nate whispered. He brought the light of his cell phone closer, and they both kneeled to read the stone face. The inscription carved into it was faded by weather and time.

"God, it's ancient." Lucy traced the letters with a trembling finger. "E . . . N. Are those initials?"

Nate leaned in closer, his face inches from Lucy's. She saw, with a quick sideways glance, that his jaw was clenched. She recognized that look; he was fascinated by their discovery.

He rubbed a patch of lichen away with his sleeve. "E-U-N," he corrected her.

Lucy sat back onto her heels, her head spinning. The inscription was familiar to her, but she wasn't sure why.

Nate trained his cell phone light on Lucy's hands, which she held clenched against her chest. She couldn't see his expression, but she felt his confusion.

"What the hell are you doing out here, Lucy?" he asked. "Why——?"

Lucy's eyes burned with tears of shame. She didn't know why she was out here, digging at a gravesite with her bare hands in the middle of the night, any more than Nate did.

"I can't say," she said.

Nate lifted the cell phone to study her face, and she recoiled like a vampire assaulted by the morning sun. "Can't . . . or won't?"

Lucy got to her feet and wiped her hands on her pants, a refusal to accept the obvious truth. Nate had taken a step backward, and she could understand why. Everything about this situation—including her—was unbelievable.

"Can we get out of here?" A convulsive shivering had taken over her body. "Please?"

"Follow me," Nate said.

Lucy let Nate and his cell phone light lead them along the overgrown path until they emerged into a clearing. She stopped in her tracks when she recognized the gnarled apple tree and the hulking house beyond it.

This was the backyard of 111 Myrtle Street, and the car parked in the driveway belonged to Nate.

They spent the five-minute drive home in silence. Lucy could only imagine how long it had taken her to make the trek from her house to the forest gravesite on foot. Had she taken the sidewalk or cut through yards? She had no memory of the barefoot walk.

Nate shut the engine off and gave her a wary sideways look. "Your parents must be heavy sleepers." He looked beyond her at the house, which was completely dark.

Lucy was relieved to see she hadn't left the front door wide open. She couldn't imagine the guilt of losing Maggie on top of everything else.

"They're in a cabin on Lake Winnipesaukee." She sighed. "My mom was gearing up to turn our house into Fort Knox before they left." She closed her eyes, suddenly bone-tired. "I kind of wish she had."

Nate cocked his head. "Fort Knox? What do you mean?"

Lucy turned to look at him. It was strange, how familiar it was to be sitting here in his car.

In her other life, she'd spent countless hours in this passenger seat, sometimes holding hands or kissing, sometimes bickering. She had the bizarre impulse to lean across the center console and bury her face against his neck, to find comfort in the familiar scent of his skin.

"This is all new to me," she said. "Sleepwalking. My mom is pretty freaked out about it."

There was so much she was leaving out—the details about how she had found herself in an unrecognizable life, the fact that she was receiving messages from some otherworldly source.

"Jesus," Nate said. He blinked hard, something he'd always done when he was processing something difficult. "I've heard of sleepwalkers rummaging in their fridges in the middle of night or taking a leak on the front lawn, but . . . this must be really scary for you."

Lucy's throat tightened at this small consolation. He wasn't looking at her as though she was a sideshow freak anymore, and that was good enough for now.

"Yeah. Hey . . . sorry I dragged you into this tonight. I must've accidentally opened a recent text and . . . it wasn't a conscious thing."

A smile flickered on Nate's face. "No need to apologize."

She reached for the car door, but he touched her arm to stop her.

"Lucy?" He cleared his throat, a nervous habit that had always grated on her nerves, *before*. "Would you feel better if you had company?"

She pretended not to notice the earnest look on Nate's face while she considered his offer.

"What about your parents?" She checked the dashboard clock and cringed. "It's three o'clock in the morning."

Nate shrugged and averted his eyes. "My parents think I'm spending the night at a friend's house. Which technically wouldn't be a lie."

Warmth crept up Lucy's neck onto her face. A riot of

conflict raged inside her head. Nate had just admitted he'd lied to his parents about his overnight plans—and the prospect of those plans involving Ashley Holt was sickening.

He'd also admitted that he considered Lucy a friend—and that he was more than willing to forfeit his other plans for her.

When she turned to look at Nate, she found he was still watching her intently.

"How do you feel about dogs?" she asked. "Big, sloppy-faced dogs?"

Nate grinned. "The bigger, the better."

Maggie gave Nate the kind of greeting she usually reserved for her favorite humans—body curved into a wagging U shape, snorting and snuffling—and he reacted exactly the way Lucy knew he would.

"Good girl," he chuckled, then glanced up at Lucy. "Must be nice having a built-in furry bodyguard."

Lucy started to say something about Nate's cat—it was a bad-ass orange tabby, every bit as territorial and protective as Maggie—but she stopped herself. As far as he knew, she'd never met his cat, or set foot inside his house for that matter.

She checked her reflection in the full-length hall mirror and gasped at what she saw: tangled hair, sweatpants and arms splattered with mud and grass stains.

"My God. I'm a wreck."

"Go ahead and clean up," Nate suggested. He

crouched beside Maggie, who leaned into his ear rubbing. "Maggie and I will hold down the fort."

LUCY SHOWERED IN RECORD TIME, BARELY AWARE OF THE mud and pine needles swirling down the drain.

When she hurried into her bedroom, dressed in a clean, oversized T-shirt and leggings, she was surprised to find Nate waiting there. He kneeled beside Maggie, one arm around her neck, his eyes on the array of concert posters lining the wall.

He glanced over his shoulder at Lucy and smiled. "I tried to keep Maggie downstairs, but she wasn't having it. Guess she was worried about you."

Lucy ran a brush through her wet hair, self-conscious. "Yeah, she's pretty needy."

Nate nodded toward the wall of posters. "KT Tunstall. You really are a fan."

She nodded. "We saw her live at the Paradise in Boston," she blurted, then caught herself. She'd dragged Nate to the show just after they'd met, and he'd been as smitten by the artist as Lucy was. "She's amazing live."

He nodded. "I can only imagine."

Lucy yawned, suddenly overcome with exhaustion.

"You should get some sleep," Nate said.

Lucy climbed into her bed and lay on her side, her hands tucked beneath her chin. Maggie nestled herself into the crook of her legs. She rested her muzzle on Lucy's hip and was snoring within seconds.

Lucy struggled to keep her eyes open. Nate surveyed

her room, hands on his hips as if he was trying to decide something.

"You really don't have to stay." Her tongue felt thick and slow. "We're fine by ourselves."

"It's not that." He sat down on the bed beside her with a sigh. "I'm just worried about it happening again and you somehow sneaking past me without noticing."

Lucy tried to respond, but she felt herself being pulled backward, her mind retreating into the dark refuge of sleep. She was dimly aware of the bed bowing under the weight of Nate's body when he laid down beside her, a human barricade between Lucy and whatever dangers lurked beyond the closed door.

THE WHISPER OF HIS BREATH AGAINST HER FACE, THE cautious brush of his lips against hers—it was all so familiar.

Nate lay on his side facing her, his fingers twined in her hair, gentle but urgent. He spoke her name so softly she wasn't sure if it was real or—

—or—

—Lucy felt the room tilt sideways, even with her eyes closed. She whimpered as it spun in the other direction, a buzzing between her ears. She opened her eyes a crack and saw her room right itself and settle.

The buzzing stopped, leaving a high-pitched whine in its place.

She propped herself up on her elbow, drugged from

sleep and disoriented. Nate curled on the bed, his knees drawn up, an elbow folded over his eyes where a stripe of early morning light blazed through the parted curtains.

In her other life, Nate had been passive, highly tuned to Lucy's physical cues. He'd never even hinted at impatience, even after months of kissing that left him breathless and trembling.

Was this version of Nate just as timid and patient?

Lucy touched her lips with her fingers. If the kiss had been real, she saw no evidence of it.

Nate shifted in his sleep and settled on his back. She studied his profile, bleary-eyed, her chest aching and heavy. He looked so serious, his brows furrowed with whatever images flickered in his subconscious mind.

Was he dreaming about her now—about the strange events of the previous night or the moments they'd shared on the catwalk?

The old Nate, the one from before, had once confessed that he dreamed about her regularly, but she'd kept her own feelings well guarded. She'd taken it all for granted—the honesty she'd been afraid to reciprocate—and now she wasn't sure she'd ever get it back.

A *ding* sounded nearby, and Lucy's first thought was of 1-11. Her cell phone lay on the dresser, and the screen was dark, powered off since their graveyard encounter.

Nate's cell phone sat on the nightstand, the screen lit with a new text. She considered reaching over his prone body to check the device, but shame stopped her. She could justify an intrusion of privacy like that in her other life—he was her boyfriend there—but here, he was a new acquaintance.

When the phone dinged again, Nate stirred and stretched. He groaned softly, and Maggie lifted her muzzle from Lucy's leg and stood up, her full-body wiggles jostling the bed. The dog buried her nose against his ear and sneezed.

Nate woke up, his eyes wide with surprise. His eyes connected with Lucy's, and her dream—or wishful thinking—came back, a sharp jab to the gut.

"Hey," he said.

"Hey." Lucy sat up, flustered. "I think someone texted you just now."

Nate studied her face for a moment, his eyes heavy-lidded. She tried to read him—was that regret in his eyes or worry?—but then he smiled.

"We did it," he said.

Lucy focused on pulling her hair into a twist, her eyes on the auburn strands between her fingers.

Was that it, then? Proof that she hadn't imagined last night's kiss?

"Good job, girl!" Nate reached for Maggie and rubbed her ears. "We did it! We kept Lucy from going rogue again."

She forced a chuckle. "Yeah . . . thanks, team."

Nate sat up, his back to Lucy, and checked his phone. When he stood up, the smile had left his eyes. "I should really get home."

She nodded. "Right. Thanks again. For everything."

She sat there, long after his footsteps retreated down

the stairs, after the front door opened and closed. She came up with a hundred different possibilities for those morning texts, but her mind kept circling back to Ashley Holt, who was probably wondering where Nate had spent the night.

27

Abby had given Lucy her personal cell phone number during their first appointment—something she did to build rapport with her patients.

Lucy suspected she was the first teenage patient to use it—especially on a Saturday morning. She had spent the last fifteen minutes pacing on the shore of the Piscataqua, but now she dialed the number, her mind made up.

When the doctor answered on the fifth ring, she sounded out of breath. "Dr. Hawkins speaking."

At the sound of Abby's voice, Lucy collapsed onto the wooden bench facing the harbor. She hadn't really expected her to pick up.

"Thank God," she breathed. "Sorry. This is Lucy McGowen—your usual Friday four o'clock?"

"Ah, Lucy of the Angel Number." Lucy could hear the smile in the doctor's voice. "Of course. Is everything okay, dear?"

Lucy let her gaze wander to the family of ducks, who

had waddled into the weeds along the shore without her noticing.

"I'm . . . okay. I just kind of needed to talk with someone who wouldn't think I'd gone off the deep end."

There was a pause on the other end, and Lucy had the fleeting impulse to hang up.

"I was actually headed out for a midday treat," Abby said. "Hot fudge makes me much more receptive to conversation. Care to join me?"

LUCY ARRIVED AT THE CONE ZONE BEFORE ABBY DID.

She spared a quick glance at the empty office adjoining the shop, where just weeks ago she'd awakened to the altered landscape of her life. The sign that had been there last time she'd looked—111 written in Sharpie—was gone.

Another sign had taken its place: *Big Changes . . . Coming SOON!*

She went inside, and the server behind the counter smiled at her. "I can take your order whenever you're ready."

Lucy approached the counter, her throat clenched against the overpowering fragrance of waffle cones. Eating seemed out of the question. "Can I get a single scoop of rainbow sherbet?"

The server obliged while Lucy watched, her heart thumping.

"The office next door," she said. "Any idea what it's going to be?"

The server rolled her eyes. "Nothing exciting. I heard it's going to be a dentist or something."

Lucy stared at the server, stone-faced.

"My boss thinks it'll be good for business." The server handed Lucy's sherbet over. "Soft foods like ice cream are a thing after oral surgery, so . . ."

The bell above the door tinkled, and Abby came in.

THEY SAT OUTSIDE AT A PICNIC TABLE WITH THEIR ICE cream, but Lucy kept her back to the vacant office. She couldn't shake the feeling that it was sending her a signal only she could hear—that it was a portal for her to travel through, back to her other life.

Abby attacked her sundae with zeal, but then she raised an eyebrow. "Okay, dear," she said. "I'll eat. You talk."

Lucy shrugged, her eyes on her melting sherbet. "This was probably a mistake."

The doctor snickered. "I personally would've gone with something with a little more pizzazz—Moose Tracks or Cookie Dough—but there's always next time."

Lucy glared at the doctor.

Abby pointed her spoon at Lucy. "I'm saying this as a friend—not as your therapist. Off the clock and off the record. You can tell me anything."

"Off the record?" Lucy squinted at Abby. "Friend to friend?"

The doctor traced an X over her heart with her spoon. "You have my word."

Lucy set her sherbet down with a shaking hand and sighed. "I don't even know where to begin."

Abby placed a gentle hand on Lucy's arm. "I find it helps to start at the beginning."

Lucy took a deep breath and did just that.

She told the doctor about the tooth extraction that had taken place at an office that now housed cobwebs and dust bunnies, and the shock of waking up to a completely revamped life.

She told her about everything that had changed: her parents' personalities, her relationships with Nate and Ella. She told her about suddenly having the dog she'd been denied in her previous life, about going from a latch-key teenager to one who was now the focus of a hyper-vigilant mother.

She laid out the details of her own transformation—how she'd once hidden her songwriting passion and musical talent from the world but had found herself in the spotlight overnight.

She confessed about all of her sleepwalking episodes, how each one had led her on a bizarre scavenger hunt orchestrated by some unknown entity.

When she finally stopped to catch her breath, she realized Abby was gaping at her, her sundae forgotten.

Lucy cringed. "Too much?"

The doctor dabbed at the corners of her mouth with a napkin, her movements calm and deliberate, but there was no mistaking the emotion in her eyes.

"Oh, Lucy!" Abby's voice wobbled, and Lucy realized

she was close to tears. "I wish you'd come to me with all of this sooner."

A bolt of fear shot through Lucy. "You're not going to out me, are you?" She could already see it in her mind's eye: the inevitable chaos culminating in Lucy's admission to an inpatient facility for troubled youth.

Abby widened her eyes. "I gave you my word, Lucy. I just hate that you've been dealing with this burden on your own."

Lucy felt tears burning behind her eyes. "I thought I was doing okay, but I've had some moments lately . . . like really scary moments."

The doctor gave her an incredulous look. "Scarier than finding yourself in a rowboat on the harbor? Scarier than uncovering an ancient grave in the woods without even knowing you were doing it?"

"There's more, Abby." Lucy felt a single tear spill over, but she didn't bother to wipe it away. "I told you about the text messages from 1-11."

Abby stared at Lucy, then reached for the charm dangling from the chain around her neck. Lucy hadn't noticed it—a silver angel—until now. "You did."

"Once, there was an actual phone call from that number." She shuddered at the memory of the haunting lullaby on the other end of the line. "With a voice on the other end. She . . . it . . . was singing."

Abby hugged her arms to her chest. "Haunted hotline," she whispered. "Wow."

"Wow is right," Lucy nodded.

"I think we have to consider that these are more than

random messages from another realm." Abby lifted her eyes to the sky, then dropped them to meet Lucy's desperate gaze. "That this is a cosmic call to action."

Lucy sighed and gathered her hair over one shoulder, then twisted it into a tight coil, around and around.

There was a part of her that had hoped the doctor would dismiss her concerns—which would give her permission to dismiss them, too. The other part was grateful that she'd validated them instead.

"It really does feel like someone—or something—is trying to get me to do something for them. For me, too."

Abby took up her ice cream and spoon again, then narrowed her eyes. "Without thinking too much, Lucy, tell me. The energy behind these messages—does it feel good or bad?"

There they were again—the full-body goosebumps. She abandoned her hair twisting to rub her arms. "Not good or bad," she said. "Just desperate . . . and sad."

Abby nodded. "Most spiritual connections are borne out of unrest," she said. "Unfinished business that keeps them stuck between."

"Between," Lucy murmured. "I know the feeling."

28

Lucy leaned against the kitchen counter and wondered if the gurgling of the coffee maker had always been this loud.

It sounded out of place at this late hour, like a songbird in the dark.

She expected her parents to return home the following day, but the night stretched before her like a jail sentence. Even Maggie, who sat with her ears perked for the rustle of the treat bag, looked worried.

While she waited for the coffee to finish brewing, she wrestled with the temptation to call Nate. He knew about her sleepwalking and the risks that went with it, and he'd even been willing to come find her in the middle of the night.

It was that willingness—and the way her mind kept wandering back to him like a homing pigeon finding its way back—that stopped her. He'd made it clear that he felt a connection with her. She felt it, too—in a way she hadn't felt it before her reincarnation as the new Lucy McGowen. She had a powerful craving to feed that connection, to see where it might lead.

But not now.

Right now, someone else was demanding her attention, sending her a call to action. Until she took that action, Lucy didn't have the time or the energy for anything else. She just wished the action—whatever that was—didn't feel so risky.

While she slept, she was at the complete mercy of some faceless metaphysical master, and she had no idea where she was going to end up next.

While she was awake, her emotions were growing increasingly raw and close to the surface. She felt close to her breaking point—physically and mentally.

The coffee maker stopped percolating, and the house fell silent. Maggie whimpered beside her—a last-ditch cry for a treat or an acknowledgment of the tension in the house.

"No sleep for me tonight, Maggie." Lucy's voice sounded too loud in the empty house. The dog nuzzled her thigh with the same enthusiasm she reserved for walks. "I've had enough nighttime adventures for one weekend."

Lucy poured herself two mugs of coffee, brewed extra strong, and headed for her bedroom. Maggie bounded up the stairs ahead of her, happy to abandon her begging for the promise of a spot on the bed.

She turned on both lamps and the overhead light, then cued up her playlist—songs designed for all-nighters and road trips—and cranked up the volume. Maggie curled up on the bed, but Lucy sat cross-legged on the hardwood floor, her back straight.

She took a gulp of coffee, then glanced at the bedside clock, which read 1:11.

She sighed. "Of course."

Her eyes wandered to the cell phone on her nightstand. She hadn't received a single text or phone call from anyone all day—not 1-11 or her parents or Nate.

Now, even with Maggie heavy-breathing on the bed, she felt utterly alone.

Lucy yawned, blinked hard, and took another sip of coffee. She paced in a tight circle, then busied herself with sliding her desk in front of the bedroom door. She wouldn't allow herself to fall asleep—*no freaking way*—but it couldn't hurt to have a backup plan.

She sat down on the bed to rub Maggie's ears, then stood up and did a few jumping jacks. Her mind was on high alert—bouncing from thought to thought like a pinball—but her eyes felt heavy. Clearly, the chaos and broken sleep of the previous night were catching up to her.

She grabbed her guitar, then sat down with it. She strummed with the song blasting over the speakers—"The Girl and The Ghost" by KT Tunstall. She tightened her throat against another yawn and sang at the top of her voice, her eyes closed.

Her eyes closed.

Her eyes—

. . .

Even with her eyes closed, Lucy knew she had walked again.

There was no glaring light beyond her eyelids—only cool darkness. Her playlist was still blasting, but it was coming from far away, above her head.

Opening her eyes only escalated her panic. She tried to stand up and the top of her head connected with solid wood. When she tried to extend her arms, she found walls on either side of her.

I'm in a box! She panted, her hands tracing the floor. It felt like cold cement, not like a box at all, a detail that gave Lucy a flicker of hope.

A verse came to her from the far reaches of her memory. *Hope is the thing with feathers . . . that perches in the soul.*

She hadn't thought of the poem since they'd studied it in freshman English.

"Emily Dickinson, right?" The sound of her own whispered voice raised goosebumps on her arms and legs. "Yep—that sounds right."

She focused on the distant music and did a quick calculation. A Talking Heads song was playing—" Burning Down the House"—which meant she was near the end of her playlist. Which meant she'd been here for quite some time.

Wherever *here* was.

She heard a queer sound—a scrabbling of claws on wood—directly above her.

Maggie?

"Maggie!" she shouted. Her voice sounded muffled in

here, but she heard the dog respond with an anxious whine. "I'm okay, girl!"

Was she okay?

She reached her hands out, a move that made her think of Blind Man's Bluff. She had grown up playing the game with Ella and a handful of other girls in the woods, but there were no breathless giggles and shrieks here—and there was no promise of daylight on the other side of a blindfold.

Her right hand plunged through something sticky—*cobweb!*—but she refused to scream. Panic would only prolong this nightmare. She wiped her fingers on her pants and reached out again. Her hands connected with something she couldn't identify with her mind's eye. It was square, wood and metal, an intricate clasp on its front side.

Above her head, Maggie circled, her claws clattering.

Lucy realized, with a mixture of relief and horror, where she was: beneath the basement stairs, in the storage compartment. She slid her hands along the box in front of her—it was more of a rectangle than a square—and knew what it was.

This was the chest full of heirloom keepsakes—the one that had held the old christening gown for so many years. She felt around for the lid latch until her fingers connected with cold metal. The padlock was missing, just as her mom had said.

She hefted the lid open with a grunt—it was much heavier than she expected—and breathed in the perfume of cedar and decay. She coughed, then felt the over-whelming need to get out of there, fast.

She pushed hard on her left, and the cubby door resisted, then swung open with a creak. Cool air rushed in, and she took a gulp of it. She crawled out of the cubby, careful to keep her head clear of the steps above her head.

From upstairs, she heard Maggie utter a single impa-tient bark.

"Coming, girl!"

She got to her feet, panting, then stopped. "Damnit."

The stairs were *right there.*

She wanted to get back upstairs with every fiber of her being—she'd be happy if she never set foot in this basement again—but one important fact remained.

She was down here for a reason.

Something had lured her down those stairs and into that storage cubby. Something had given her access to that locked heirloom chest. Denial would only prolong her agony. She could pretend she was in control of the situation, but she would only be kidding herself. Ignoring these calls for action was not an option.

"Okay, okay!" she hissed.

Her eyes had adjusted to the dark just enough for her to find the under-stairs cubby door again. She scooted back inside on her knees, cursing, and let her hands slide over the lip of the heirloom chest. She felt around blindly, her heart galloping inside her ribcage.

She felt fabric—lace and wool—and then her fingers grazed something stiff. The dimensions reminded her of a book, without the thickness or weight of one. She drew it out without hesitation, then closed the lid, her mind infused with a strange knowing.

This was what she'd come for.

She closed the cubby door behind her and stood up, the mystery souvenir pressed to her chest. Maggie had abandoned her top-of-the-stairs patrol, and aside from the low rumble of the water heater, the basement was silent.

The base of her skull tingled. She couldn't see a thing down here—her sleepwalking self hadn't bothered with the hallway light this time—but she felt something watching her.

Watching . . . and waiting.

Lucy was suddenly awash with adrenaline, and she bolted for the basement stairs, a scream stuck in her throat. She stumbled on the first step and cracked her shin on the edge of a stair before she scrambled to the main floor and down the dark hallway.

She didn't stop until she made it to her bedroom, Maggie bouncing behind her, excited by this middle-of-the-night game of chase.

Her room was just as she'd left it—music pounding and lights on—but one of her mugs had toppled, a brown pool spread around it. The desk she'd carefully pinned against her door was shoved to one side.

Lucy silenced her playlist, then collapsed onto her bed to study her basement trophy. It was a photograph printed on thick cardboard, the squared edges softened by time.

The black-and-white image was of a young woman,

her dark hair woven into a long braid. She held a bundle in her arms—a swaddled infant—but there wasn't a trace of a smile on her pale face.

The photo was faded, the details blurred by the passing years, but there was something familiar about the defiant set of the mother's jaw, the challenge in her eyes.

Her parents would return home later that afternoon, but she wasn't eager to confess what she'd retrieved, sleeping or not. They'd finally stopped treating her like an explosive substance. A second breach of the heirloom chest would bring a renewed interest in keeping Lucy under lock and key—or worse.

She put the photo on her nightstand, then lay back on her bed without bothering to turn the lights out. She wasn't sure she could deal with darkness after what she'd just been through, with whatever presence she'd felt in the basement lingering in the back of her mind.

"Good girl, Maggie," she whispered, one hand on her dog's velvety back. It was her way of asking the dog to stay there beside her—and a half-assed promise to return the favor.

As if the choice was hers to make.

29

Lucy woke with a start.

She glanced at Maggie, curious about whether a noise had jerked her out of sleep, but the dog was still snoring, her barrel chest rising and falling.

As Lucy stretched, she saw something darkening her pillow on her left, an object in her peripheral vision. She turned her head, then bolted upright.

The old photo—the one she'd snagged during last night's basement adventure—was propped there, face down. She gasped, and Maggie lifted her head, instantly on guard.

Lucy would have sworn she'd left the photo on her nightstand before she'd dozed off. There was no way she would have left it on her pillow to risk crushing it.

"Relax—you moved it while you were half-asleep." Her whispered proposal was weak, she knew that, but the alternative was unthinkable. If *she* hadn't moved it—awake or sleeping—then someone else had.

The memory of the presence she'd felt in the basement, watchful and silent, chilled her.

She bent to study the back of the photo, which was
inscribed with slanting, elegant cursive. The ink was dark
and precise—nothing like the time-worn image on the
front. The previous night felt fuzzy, like the remnants of a
dream, but she remembered turning the cardboard over a
few times, front to back. If the handwriting had been
there, she would have seen it.

But it hadn't—and *she* hadn't.

Her eyes skated over the words, which were printed in
another language: *thiodhlaic e e air an eilean.* She didn't
realize what she had done—translated the inscription in
her mind without a moment of hesitation—until the
words morphed into a jumble of nonsensical letters
before her eyes.

She typed the phrase into her phone's search engine,
her chest tight, desperate to confirm what she already
knew it said. She didn't release her breath until the Scots-
Gaelic translation popped up.

It was just as she'd read it the first time: *He buried him
on the island.*

"Holy shit," she whispered.

Maggie watched her with rapt attention, her ears
cocked. She pressed her nose to the space behind Lucy's
ear, snuffling, then bounced off the bed and danced in a
tight circle.

"Okay, okay," Lucy said.

She let Maggie lead the way down the stairs and out
the back door, her limbs on autopilot. She stood there,

looking out, but it wasn't her backyard she saw in her mind's eye. It was the rocky island set between the Piscataqua River and the sea, home of the ancient lighthouse—the one her rowboat had drifted toward while she'd hovered in some strange limbo between wakefulness and sleep.

Who was *he*, and who had he buried on the island?

The tiny bundle in the young mother's arms in the photograph?

Who, then, occupied the overgrown forest grave—the one she'd unearthed the other night while her brain slept?

She didn't notice the female cardinal perched on the fencepost until it called out with a loud, metallic *chip!* It looked at Lucy, cocked its crested head, then flew off.

Her thoughts circled back to the forest graveyard, where she and Nate had discovered the age-worn stone bearing the initials EUN.

But what if they weren't initials at all?

Lucy pulled her phone out to do another search. This time, she typed *Scots-Gaelic translation to English—eun.*

The result came back instantly, a sucker punch to Lucy's gut.

Eun was Scots-Gaelic for *bird.*

AFTER EVERYONE ELSE HAD LEFT HISTORY CLASS, LUCY hesitated at Mr. Dillinger's desk.

The teacher gave his eyes a vigorous rub, as though his lesson about the Emancipation Proclamation had left him as rummy as it had left his students. He perked up when he saw what Lucy held in her hands.

She'd carefully slid the old photograph between the pages of a textbook to protect it, because she didn't dare leave it at home, where her mom might find it and go berserk. Returning it to the heirloom chest was out of the question; she wasn't sure she could bring herself to set foot in the basement again.

Mr. Dillinger slid his reading glasses on and grinned. "What have we here, Miss McGowen?"

There was no turning back. Lucy handed the photograph over.

He whistled under his breath, impressed. "Wow. This is quite a relic."

She took a cautious step forward. "Old, huh?" She cleared her throat. "Any idea how old, Mr. Dillinger?"

The teacher pursed his lips and slid his fingers over the edge of the thick cardboard. Then, to Lucy's surprise, he sniffed it.

"It's a *carte-de-visite*," he said.

Lucy frowned. "A what?"

"A photograph printed on heavy cardstock," Mr. Dillinger explained. "They switched to paper sometime after the mid-eighteen-hundreds because it was cheaper. Before that, glass and metal tintypes were the go-to."

Lucy nodded, an attempt at nonchalance. "Interesting."

Mr. Dillinger tilted the photo into the light for a better look. "The sepia tone process you see here was used to make the image more stable and longer lasting. This one is very well preserved."

He turned the photo over. "No clues on the back, but my best amateur guess is that it dates back to around the turn of the century."

He handed it back with a smile and took his reading glasses off.

"Thanks, Mr. Dillinger," Lucy said.

She tucked the photograph into the textbook, and she didn't slide it back out again until she had retreated into the hallway, her pulse whooshing in her ears.

Her teacher had confirmed her suspicions—that the photograph dated back to around the same time Aoife Cormac had given birth to baby Calum.

But that wasn't what made her hands tremble as she turned the stiff cardboard over. Her breath caught when she saw it. The back of the photo was now blank, just as Mr. Dillinger had said.

The message she'd seen written there earlier—*he buried him on the island*—had been meant for her eyes only.

30

Lucy felt conflicted when she saw her mom's car parked in the driveway after school.

She was relieved that she wouldn't have to spend another night alone in the house. The trade-off was the loss of quiet time to think about everything that had happened in the last few days.

In this life, she had newfound confidence, but she'd also gained a turn-of-the-century tyrant who had recruited Lucy to arrange a long overdue reunion.

All day, she'd been wrestling with the temptation to come clean with Nate about the details that were surfacing like a slow-to-develop photograph.

How would that conversation look?

How could she explain that she had traded a bad tooth for a new life?

That she had essentially been reincarnated in her own body?

Abby, with her office scented by incense and sage, had

felt like a safe bet. She didn't want to scare the new Nate off—not when she was just getting to know him again.

Lucy found her mom in the kitchen. After years of foraging and fending for herself, the sight of her mom bustling at the stove was still unnerving.

"Hi, honey." Her mom glanced over her shoulder, then abandoned her cooking to give Lucy a hug.

She registered her mom's scent—a floral perfume as unfamiliar as her embrace.

"Hey," Lucy said. "How was your anniversary adventure?"

"It was wonderful." Joanne wiped her fingers on her apron, and that's when Lucy noticed the furrow between her eyebrows. "I can't remember the last time your dad and I had quality time together, just the two of us."

"Yeah?" Lucy pulled her lunch sack out of her backpack, a preemptive strike. The last thing she wanted was her mom rummaging through her stuff, where she might stumble on the old photograph. "When did you guys get back?"

"Couple of hours ago. We made a quick stop at the pharmacy." Joanne avoided her eyes as she dug in her gargantuan purse. She pulled out a plastic pill bottle and shook it like a mini maraca.

Lucy went cold. "What's that?"

"The doctor thought this might help with your nighttime issues."

Lucy crossed her arms. "Abby didn't mention anything to me about medication."

"Another doctor." Her mom gave the pill bottle

another shake, her face hopeful. "I thought it might be worth a try, just to see if it might keep things under control."

She had seen the way her mom dropped her eyes when she said the word *things*. By things, she clearly meant Lucy.

She took a step backward and glared at her mom. "What is it?"

Joanne set the bottle down and turned back to the stove. She stirred whatever was simmering in the pot. When she spoke again, her voice was barely audible. "Klonopin."

Lucy stalked over to the counter and picked up the pill bottle. "Klonopin? Isn't that a heavy-duty sedative?"

"It's commonly used to treat anxiety, but it's reported to curb sleepwalking in a high percentage of patients."

Lucy scoffed in disbelief. "Mom, did you see the side effects listed on this insert? Seizures, hallucinations, shallow breathing, extreme mood swings, paranoia, suicidal thoughts—"

Joanne held her hands up. "They have to list even the most unlikely side effects, honey."

Lucy blinked back tears. "No way." She shook her head. "I am not taking this."

Joanne pointed a finger at her, her eyes narrowed. "This isn't up to you," she said. "We're your parents, and we can't have you wandering off in the middle of the night. I've read some horrific stories about sleepwalkers and what they're capable of."

Lucy recoiled as though her mom had slapped her

face. "So that's it? You're afraid I'm going to murder you and Dad in your sleep?"

"I never said that," Joanne sputtered.

"You didn't need to."

"We'll talk about this more when your dad gets back from walking Maggie." Lucy heard the warning in her mom's tone: *you can say no to me—but that won't fly with Dad.* "I ordered a home security system, too, but they can't install it until Friday."

Lucy lifted her chin, defiant. "Wow, Mom. Sedated and incarcerated—problem solved, right?"

"It's for your own safety, honey."

She stalked out of the room, snagged her ukulele case from the living room, and made a beeline for the front door.

"Where do you think you're going?" Joanne called out.

"While you've been plotting about ways to control me, I've been practicing for tomorrow's talent show."

She yanked the front door open, her throat locked against the sob threatening to escape.

"Your dad and I have front row tickets." Joanne approached, her arms outstretched. "We're so excited to see what you're going to do."

Lucy shot her mom a scathing look. "Haven't you heard, Mom? I'm very unpredictable these days. I think it would be safer if you kept your distance."

She heard her mom open the screen door as she hopped on her bike and pedaled away, tears wetting her checks. She refused to give her the satisfaction of looking back.

A moment later, she almost collided with Ella.

Her friend was crossing the sidewalk, a grocery bag cradled in each arm. Lucy braked hard, tires screeching on the pavement, and her bike skidded sideways.

"Where's the fire?" Ella exclaimed. "And why do you look like someone peed in your spilled milk?"

Lucy wasn't sure if it was the comforting Ella-ism that defused her anger——or the close call——and she didn't care.

She straddled her bike and managed a smile. "Sorry, El. My mom is being a colossal pain in the ass today."

She felt guilty the moment the words were out of her mouth, but Ella didn't even flinch.

"Bummer."

Lucy glanced at the car parked at the curb and cocked her head. "Ella McElroy, did you just drive to the grocery store without a driver's license?"

Ella shrugged and grinned. "I have a valid permit——close enough, right? Somebody had to stock the fridge."

That's when Lucy saw the exhaustion behind Ella's faltering smile.

"Need some help with putting those away?"

Ella rolled her eyes. "About time you made yourself useful."

Following Ella into the house felt like entering a different time zone. The living room was all shadows, the curtains shut tight against the afternoon sunshine.

The kitchen was quiet but tidy—the drying rack lined with dishes, the counters wiped clean. Lucy didn't need to ask Ella who had been keeping things so neat and organized. Today marked her third missed day of school in a week.

"House looks nice," Lucy offered.

Ella began pulling groceries out of bags. "Yeah. Looks can be deceiving."

Lucy reached a hand out to squeeze Ella's arm. "Still bad?"

Ella opened her mouth to answer, but then Mrs. McElroy breezed into the kitchen, humming under her breath.

"Good morning, beautiful girls," she crooned. She fetched herself a coffee mug, then filled it.

Lucy glanced at Ella, who had resumed her grocery unpacking, her face frozen with hope.

"Coffee is probably cold by now, Mom," she said. "Might want to warm it up."

Her mom put her cup in the microwave, still humming, then went to plant a kiss on Ella's forehead.

"My sweet girl," she said. "What would I do without you?"

She gathered her car keys and lifted her purse strap to her shoulder. Lucy gave her a quick appraisal: full makeup, coiffed hair, dress and heels.

"Going somewhere?" Ella asked.

"I'm in the mood for some retail therapy," her mom sang out. She strode into the living room and drew the curtains open, flooding the room with bright light. "Looks like a gorgeous day, girls! You should really get outside and enjoy it."

Ella and Lucy exchanged a baffled look.

"Mom—your coffee," she called out, but Mrs. McElroy was already opening the front door.

She blew them a kiss and beamed. "You know what? I think I'll hit that new coffee shop on Main Street. They have the most delectable scones. I am ravenous!"

She left, her heels clicking on the front walk, her hair bouncing behind her.

Ella sank down onto a kitchen chair, her shoulders slumped. Lucy tried to read her expression, which had gone from shocked to blank.

"You okay, El?" she asked.

A smile flickered on Ella's face, and she sighed. "Yeah," she said. "On the bright side, I think I can safely say I'll see you at school tomorrow."

Lucy felt the sudden urge to cry—for her friend's pain, and for her own—and she swallowed hard.

"Think you'll be up for the talent show tomorrow night?" she ventured.

Ella's smile was genuine. "Do wild horses fly?"

Lucy returned her smile. She wasn't sure what she had done to deserve a friend like Ella McElroy, but she was grateful for her presence.

The *before* was a distant memory, the *after* was stranger than fiction—but Ella was there for all of it, constant and unwavering.

31

Lucy opened her eyes to a surprising view of her own bedroom ceiling.

She had reluctantly gone to bed, certain she would wake up in an unfamiliar place, a human pawn in someone else's twisted game.

She unclenched her fists and willed her muscles to relax. She'd managed to sneak up to bed last night without running into her parents—and without a continuation of the dreaded Klonopin conversation.

Even without medication, she had not walked.

She lay there, blinking up at the smooth paint above her—the spot that, in her other-life bedroom, had cracked and peeled from neglect.

Outward signs of neglect were hard to find here, in this life.

Outside, a mockingbird let loose with a string of descending chirps, again and again, a one-sided conversation. Lucy turned her face to the window and closed her eyes, listening, but the mockingbird had already abandoned its brazen melody for a simple, one-note call.

She'd always admired mockingbirds—their vocal prowess, their versatility. They were known to sing well after sundown, sometimes by the light of a full moon. They weren't much to look at—slender and grey—but some males boasted a repertoire of two hundred songs.

Average looks with a hidden superpower, a knack for adapting and blending. Just like Lucy.

She sat up in bed, yawning, then gasped.

Her mind scrambled to decode the impossibility before her sleep-blurred eyes. The computer desk was right where she'd slid it before bed, blocking her bedroom door, not a paper out of place on its surface.

A shovel—the relic she'd shared a rowboat with not long ago—leaned against it, spade side down.

She got out of bed, slowly, dimly aware that the mockingbird outside was on to bigger and better things—a raucous shrieking that matched Lucy's thoughts.

The door barricade implied she hadn't left the room last night, but something had been in there with her.

Not something—*someone.*

Someone with a name: Aoife Cormac.

Lucy's legs buckled for a moment, but then she made her way to the desk. The shovel's wooden handle felt icy, as though it had just been outside in the cool morning air.

When her cell phone chimed on the desk, she let her eyes drop to the lit screen to confirm what she already knew.

It was a message from 1-11. *Bring him to me tonight.*

Lucy backed away from the desk, her nostrils flared with the effort of quieting her breath.

The talent show was tonight. Maybe, if she left her phone sitting on the desk, if she pretended she hadn't gotten the message, she could buy herself some time.

The phone chimed again with another message from 1-11, and Lucy craned forward to see the message on her screen.

Let us rest.

She stared at her phone, her fingers curled against her throat. Her phone chimed again and again and again.

Let us rest.

Let us rest.

Let us rest.

She reached for her phone and powered it off with a trembling hand, then sat on her bed, her knees drawn to her chest.

At some point, the mockingbird outside her window had fallen silent—or flown away—leaving Lucy alone with her pounding heart.

32

Backstage, Lucy took a deep breath to quiet the gnawing inside her rib cage.

She hadn't had this feeling in weeks—not since her other life—but she recognized it. It was stage fright, the very thing that had kept the old Lucy confined to her bedroom with her guitar, the thing that kept her well out of the spotlight.

The deep breath helped.

She wiped her palms on her skirt and adjusted the strap of her guitar for the hundredth time and checked the wall clock on the far side of the stage. The show would start in fifteen minutes.

A giggling swarm of dancers spilled into the stage right queue, all of them dressed in matching black bodysuits, their facial expressions exaggerated by heavy makeup. Ashley Holt hovered at the center of this mass—the unspoken nucleus of the dance team's impermeable membrane.

Lucy felt another pang of anxiety. She'd seen the dance team in action before, all muscled limbs and curves, a perfectly synchronized display of physical perfection.

How the hell was she supposed to follow that? She imagined herself out there under the glare of the spotlight, drab and colorless, an imposter.

"Nothing but a mockingbird," Lucy whispered. She crept forward to peer out past the curtain, where the auditorium was almost packed to capacity. Her throat tightened, threatening to cut off her breath and her voice. "Totally unoriginal."

Someone tugged on her hair, and she turned to find Nate standing there, his own guitar dangling on its strap, a plastic guitar pick clenched between his teeth. He pulled it out and grinned at her.

"I've been looking for you everywhere," he said.

"I don't belong here," Lucy blurted. Heat radiated from beneath her shirt collar, and her hair clung to her clammy neck.

Nate took a step forward and ducked his head to look into her wide eyes. "Of course you do," he said. "This is where they told us to line up."

Lucy dragged her eyes away from Nate's face. Her gaze settled on Ashley, who was watching them from a distance, bemused.

"No." She fanned herself with her hands. "I mean here. This show. This version of things. I'm a total fraud."

Nate led her away from the performance queue to a

shadowed corner behind the stage. It smelled like paint and electricity and sweat, but it was private.

"Lucy, breathe," he said. "You deserve to be here on this stage."

She gulped air and nodded. Nate held one of her hands between his, and the gentle pressure was strangely calming. He watched her face, his eyes bright and alert.

"Okay," she said. "I'm okay. I just had a moment."

"Happens to the best of us." He gave her hand a squeeze, then let go.

She forced a smile. "Psssh. You're one to talk. You haven't even broken a sweat."

Nate ran his hands through his hair, his gaze far away. He seemed to be wrestling with something more troubling than stage fright.

"That's where you're wrong, Lucy," he said. He brought his focus back to her face, only this time his smile had vanished. "I barely slept last night."

"You'll be great out there," she insisted.

Nate shook his head and lowered his eyes. "I had a nightmare, only it felt more like déjà vu." He sighed. "It was about you."

She recoiled, secretly flattered. "Me?"

"In the dream, you were fading out—and then I could barely remember you. Like you hadn't actually been here at all."

Lucy swallowed. "That's quite a dream."

His mouth trembled, and she saw the tendons on his neck tighten. "You're not going anywhere, are you?"

She opened her mouth to respond, then closed it. She

wished she could answer that question with complete confidence, but if she'd learned anything over the last month, it was that she wasn't in control of anything.

"I'm not planning on it," she finally said.

Nate stared at her for a long moment. Then he stepped closer, one hand on his guitar, the other hand reaching for her. He tucked a wisp of auburn hair behind her ear, his touch a whisper against her cheekbone.

"That's really good news," he murmured.

He bent, his guitar clacking against hers, and slid his fingers into her hair. It was so familiar—the warmth of his breath, the soft brush of his lips against hers—but the electric zing in the pit of her stomach was all new.

His voice in her ear—*Lucy*—was like a drug, and she swayed on her feet.

She looked up. "But I thought . . . aren't you and Ashley—"

Nate shook his head. "We're just friends." He leaned in again, his guitar colliding with hers again, the twanging of their strings discordant. "We talked about it."

"Nate!" The stage director appeared, waving frantically. "Dude, you're on!"

Nate backed away, his eyes pleading. "Promise me you won't go anywhere!"

He disappeared around the corner, and Lucy stood there, wondering what he'd meant by that—and whether it was a promise she could make.

. . .

EVERYTHING AFTER THAT—NATE'S PERFORMANCE, THE din of audience applause, waiting for her turn to go on—was a blur.

The moments crawled by, but the emcee caught Lucy off guard when he announced her name.

By the time she made her way to the stool in the center of the stage, the auditorium had fallen silent. Lucy squinted into the spotlight and listened to her own heartbeat, a metronome set at the wrong, chaotic pace.

The spotlight had turned the first several rows into a shapeless silhouette, but she knew her parents were out there somewhere, watching her, rooting for her to redeem herself.

She closed her eyes and thought about Nate telling her to breathe, telling her she deserved this moment, and her pulse slowed to a steady march. She felt the strings, stretched taut beneath her calloused fingertips.

She adjusted the standing microphone in front of her, and it let out a sharp squeal of audio feedback. The sound cut straight to her reptilian mind, the part that knew how to tune everything else out—the hundreds of eyes on her, the trembling of her limbs, even Nate.

She breathed.

She began, her fingers plucking the strings with ease. These weren't the same chords she'd been practicing for weeks. There was something familiar about the notes; she recognized their beauty the way a passenger admires a pretty view from a train, only she knew she had no control over the route or the destination.

She was just along for the ride.

Panic flared inside her, sudden and bright, and her fingers slid from the strings with a cacophonous clang. A murmur rose from the audience, a shifting of feet.

Lucy lifted a hand to shield her eyes from the spotlight, her heart pounding, and considered bolting toward the safety of backstage. She glanced right and found Nate standing there. When their eyes connected, he nodded and gave her a double thumbs-up.

She lowered her chin and closed her eyes, reminded herself to breathe. The feeling came back—a prickling at the back of her brain, a need to finish the song—and her fingers resumed their plucking.

When she opened her mouth to sing the lyrics—each line introducing itself like a stranger—she felt the hairs on the back of her neck stand up. This was her voice, but the feeling behind the words belonged to someone else.

She didn't fight it.

She knew she was no longer in charge, and there was something comforting about that fact.

It wasn't until she began singing the last verse that her eyes found a familiar face in the audience, pale as the moon, long dark hair woven into a thick braid over her shoulder.

Ava.

Lucy's voice rang out. "Child of my heart, sleep calmly and well at night, and be happy."

Ava held her gaze, her forehead crinkled with emotion. Lucy felt all of it—a mother's grief and longing—and it was enough to make her want to break down and cry.

She kept singing.

"I'm by your side praying blessings on you . . . hush-a-bye, baby, and sleep for now."

The last note hung in the air, and Lucy felt a tear trace a path down her cheek.

The silence gave way to applause—a roar punctuated by whistles and calls—and Lucy lowered her guitar and closed her eyes.

"Thank you," she whispered into the microphone.

She stood up on quaking legs and gave a small bow, then let her eyes drift back to Ava's seat.

It was empty.

Lucy strode backstage, head down, through the crowd of performers waiting for the judges to make their decision.

Ashley's voice floated by: "Right? Who sings a freaking lullaby at a high school talent show?"

Lucy bolted for the auditorium door, her guitar bouncing against her hip, her mind made up. She had something important to tend to—and it couldn't wait another minute.

"Lucy!" Nate caught up with her, breathing hard.

She turned to face him. "I have to go."

His eyes were wide with surprise and admiration. "You were magic out there."

"Thanks, Nate, but I really have to—"

"They haven't announced the winners yet, but I think we all know who won first place."

Lucy wiped her face with her sleeve. "I'm sorry," she said. "There's someone who needs my help."

Nate held his hands up. "Let me go get my guitar," he said. "I'll come with you."

She shook her head, and she winced when she saw the disappointment on Nate's face. "I have to do this alone."

Nate gave her a searching look, then nodded. "Okay. You know where to find me, I guess."

Lucy reached for his hand, and he took it, his eyes hopeful.

"We'll find each other."

LUCY COULDN'T BELIEVE SHE HADN'T SEEN IT SOONER.

A quick Google search on her phone confirmed it: *Aoife* was the Gaelic version of the name *Ava*.

She powered her phone off, then pocketed it and set out for home, her mind racing. Her parents would be looking for her after the judges made their announcement, and it wouldn't be long before they realized she was nowhere to be found—another thirty minutes, by her estimation. That would allow her enough time to get home and grab the spade, but then what?

Accomplishing what was being asked of her would take a Herculean effort. She wasn't sure she was up for it, physically or mentally.

Lucy walked as fast as her legs would carry her, huffing and puffing. "The name thing is just a coincidence." She looked around to make sure no one was witnessing her bizarre, solo argument. "There is *no way* you shared your lunch table with a ghost."

She chuckled to herself, though she had that feeling in her throat that usually preceded crying.

This wasn't just *any* ghost—it was a grief-stricken mother who'd died of a broken heart a hundred years ago. An ancient ghost who clearly wouldn't take no for an answer. One who had lost her child, then lost her voice.

Lucy stopped in her tracks and held her hands up. "Why me?"

She stood there, her face turned to the sky, where an almost-full moon played hide-and-seek behind wisps of cloud.

A pair of headlights swept over her, jolting her out of her despair. She started walking ahead, her eyes lowered. Her questions would have to wait. Now was the time for action.

The headlights brightened, and a car pulled up behind her and stopped. She glanced over her shoulder, anxiety making her fingertips tingle. Had her parents found her, even with her phone's location turned off?

"Luce!" The girl leaning out the passenger side window beamed. "Dude, seriously? Way to ghost on me."

Lucy felt frozen to the sidewalk. "Did you say ghost?"

Ella laughed. "Are you allergic to winning or something? When we left, they were checking all the bathrooms for you. Come on—get in!"

Lucy had the wild urge to turn and run, but it passed. If she could convince Ella and her mom to drop her at the house, she could get in and out before her parents left the high school.

"Yeah, thanks."

Lucy climbed into the back seat, and Ella's mom swiveled to give her a dazzling smile.

"Honey, you sang like an angel up there." She extended a hand and refused to retract it until Lucy gave her a dazed high-five. "You honestly had the entire place in tears."

"My mom speaks the truth." Ella nodded, then rolled her eyes skyward. "I must have tried to call you a hundred times just now. I was actually starting to worry."

Lucy bit her lower lip. "Sorry, El. I turned my phone off for the show." She hated lying to her friend, but what choice did she have? "I wasn't feeling well afterwards, so I ran outside for some fresh air. Think I might be coming down with something."

"Dang," Ella sighed. "I was going to ask you to spend the night, a mini-celebration of your amazing performance. Tonight would have been a good night for it."

Lucy met Ella's eyes and knew what she meant by that—her mom was up for it today, but there were no guarantees beyond that.

"Sorry, El."

Ella shrugged. "No skin off my back."

"Off my nose," Lucy corrected.

She was tempted to take Ella up on her sleepover offer—to pretend she wasn't the target of some spiritual bully. Eating popcorn and painting nails sounded far superior to digging for bones in the dark, alone.

She had just opened her mouth to say something when she spotted the figure standing in the middle of the road, her defiant posture and long, dark braid suddenly ablaze in their headlights. She let out a strangled cry—there was no time to scream—as they collided with her.

Lucy collapsed onto her side, her seat belt straining, her eyes wide. In the front seat, Ella and her mom bobbed their heads to the music on the radio, oblivious.

She bolted upright and swiveled to look through the rear window. She scanned the road for the crumpled shape of a person, broken limbs splayed on concrete, as the moon slid out from behind the clouds again.

She was still there, a silhouette standing in the center of the road, the expression on her face unreadable as they left her behind. Ella hadn't seen her, and neither had her mom, and they didn't notice that Lucy had flattened herself against the back seat, breathless with shock.

They couldn't possibly know that the night was far from over for Lucy, who had been chosen, like it or not.

33

When Lucy got home, the front door opened an inch before it met with solid resistance.

Her heart seized up, but then she heard a wet snort and the ticking of claws on hardwood. "Hey, Maggie," she said. "Good girl."

Lucy went inside and closed the door behind her. Aside from Maggie's tap dancing, the house was quiet, but it wouldn't be for long. It was only a matter of time before her parents pulled up with a tirade of questions about why she'd left the talent show without them.

Her eyes drifted to the stairway that led upstairs to her bedroom, where the rusty shovel waited. She'd stashed it in her closet, along with a backpack of essentials for her mission: flashlight, water bottle, work gloves.

Maggie perched on the bed and watched Lucy trade her talent show skirt for dark jeans, a hoodie and Doc Martens. When she shouldered her backpack and picked up the rusted spade, the dog leapt from the bed and wagged her rear end from side to side.

"I'll be right back," Lucy said. It was a lie, of course—the undertaking she faced would take hours, if she succeeded at all—but Maggie's eyes remained hopeful and alert.

She hurried downstairs, patted her back pocket to make sure she had her phone and house keys, then hesitated at the front door. Maggie had followed close behind, and now she sat down beside her, ears cocked. She looked up at Lucy, expectant.

"Not this time, Maggie."

The dog protested with a gutteral sound—*unk unk unk*—which threatened to escalate into a howl.

Lucy glanced out the front window—no sign of car headlights yet, thank God—and made up her mind. "Fine."

She hurried into the kitchen to dash off a note to her parents—*Walking Maggie to burn off some adrenaline! Don't wait up!*—then found the dog's collar and leash. "Don't make me regret this."

Lucy secured the collar while Maggie writhed in ecstasy. "Easy," she whispered—more to herself than to her dog. She hadn't even left the house yet, but she felt like she couldn't catch her breath.

Once they were outside, Maggie seemed to sense that Lucy was on a mission. She trotted ahead of her at a steady pace, only squatting to pee once, her head on a swivel.

They made it to the park in thirty minutes, and they

didn't pass a single car. Lucy's phone was still off—her location dark—but she halfway expected her mom to have the police combing the streets for her by now.

The rowboat was in its place on the shore, its weathered hull canted to one side.

Lucy closed her eyes and whimpered at the sight of it. "Thank God."

She released Maggie from the leash and went to investigate the boat. The dog took a few laps of brackish water, then sneezed.

"Oars!" Lucy's exclamation prompted Maggie to do a gleeful water dance.

She had been prepared to use the shovel as a makeshift paddle—like the last time she'd found herself drifting toward the lighthouse. Since then, someone had fitted the corroded oar locks with aluminum oars.

Lucy looked around, her eyes wide. "Someone . . . or something?"

She loaded her backpack into the boat, along with the shovel, then unwound the thick rope connecting the boat to its post.

She gave a whistle, and Maggie abandoned her water frolicking and bounded up to the boat. She sprang into its hull effortlessly, circled around, then bounced back onto the shore.

"Come on, girl!" Lucy patted the side of the boat. "Up up!"

Maggie snorted, pranced in place, then darted back into the water to pursue her own doggie agenda.

Lucy checked the parking lot, her pulse racing. What

had she been thinking—dragging this furry clown along with her on such a daunting mission?

She didn't have time to get her back home; her parents were likely there by now. Leaving the dog unattended on the beach alone was not an option—not even with her leash tied to something.

"Shit shit shit," Lucy hissed.

For the tenth time tonight, she felt close to tears.

She gave the rowboat a shove toward the water, her boots squelching in the tidal mud, her breath coming in harsh puffs. She'd seen plenty of moms pull the same stunt at the playground—the old fake-out—but Maggie was a dog, not a toddler.

"See ya," she called over her shoulder. She pulled her legs into the hull of the boat, her hands gripping the sides, her rear end landing squarely on the rotting seat.

Maggie splashed behind her, back and forth, then let out a desperate howl.

Lucy kept her eyes straight ahead, her gaze fixed on the darkened lighthouse on the island ahead. When she heard Maggie pouncing through the water toward her, she crouched low to steady herself. The dog leapt into the boat, claws skidding on wet wood. The rowboat rocked from side to side, the water rippling around them.

"Good girl, Maggie!" Lucy patted the floor of the boat, and Maggie sat facing the front, tongue lolling out, a comical masthead on a questionable vessel. "Let's do this."

Lucy synced her breathing with her rowing, focused on the task at hand. She imagined a spotlight sweeping across the harbor and settling on her boat, a police officer's megaphoned command to turn around and return to shore. The faster she pulled the rowboat up onto the rocky island and tucked it out of view, the better.

After what felt like an eternity, the rowboat scraped the rocky bottom, and Maggie abandoned the hull with a graceful, arching jump. She picked her way along the shore and began her snuffling investigation.

Lucy dragged the rowboat onto the shore, her boots slipping on the moss-covered rocks. It hadn't occurred to her that the shovel would be all but useless on the island, which was more granite than soil.

Maggie nudged her thigh with her mud-crusted muzzle, and she sighed. "You don't happen to have a jackhammer, do you, girl?"

The dog wagged her stubby tail, then stood at attention, listening.

Lucy looked around. She couldn't hear anything but the water lapping at the shore, the scuttling of unseen hermit crabs, the wet crackling of clams digging their tunnels.

"What is it, girl?" she whispered.

Maggie set off, whimpering, toward the lighthouse. The structure loomed a hundred feet off, its base hidden by a tangle of shrubs. From the far shore, it had seemed stately, but from this distance, under the full moon's light, it looked like a tired victim of decay and neglect.

"Wait up, Maggie!" Lucy scrambled over the shore. She swore under her breath, her backpack slapping behind her, the shovel a makeshift walking stick.

She could hear it now—the sound that had drawn Maggie. She held her breath and listened until she could pinpoint the source of the repetitive noise. The lighthouse door was askew, dangling by one corroded hinge, the weathered wood clapping in the breeze. It looked one storm shy of being carried off by the wind.

Maggie trotted toward it, her head lowered.

"Stay, Maggie!" she called out.

The dog hesitated to sniff the gap beneath the broken door and the ground—but not for long. She disappeared into the darkness inside.

"Maggie!" Lucy yelled.

She tried to run the last few steps to the lighthouse, but her shoe wedged between two rocks and she went down hard on one knee. She cried out as the shovel clattered to the ground.

From inside the lighthouse, Maggie let out a single, muffled bark. Was she reacting to Lucy's cry—or something else?

Lucy reclaimed the shovel, scrabbled over the rocks, and crouched before the lighthouse door. She silenced the wooden clapping with one hand, then yanked the rusted doorknob hard. She stepped aside as the door came off the remaining hinge and crashed to the rocks.

She lifted her chin and strained to listen for Maggie.

Nothing.

She took a deep breath, wrinkled her nose at the stench of damp wood and mildew, then rummaged in her backpack for her flashlight.

"Damn dog!"

The truth was, Maggie provided a welcome distraction from the task she faced, and she was grateful for it. She couldn't imagine being here on this dark island alone.

She stepped into the lighthouse, the round beam from her flashlight jiggling on the crumbling wall. The concrete floor was littered with dried grass, bug carcasses and leaves carried in by the wind.

Straight ahead, a rickety wrought iron staircase spiraled up and up until it disappeared on another level.

She listened for the metallic clicking of Maggie's claws on the staircase—for any sign of the dog at all—but heard only a muffled scratching that made her think of rodents. She shuddered, her light bouncing on the floor.

"Maggie?" Her voice echoed inside the octagon walls.

Three minutes had passed since the dog had disappeared into the lighthouse. Maybe more.

"I'm coming up," Lucy called—more as a warning to whatever might lurk in the shadows, rodents or otherwise.

She followed the trembling beam of light upward, one hand on the wobbly railing, her neck craned. Her footsteps clanged on the metal steps. They were narrow and steep, the kind of challenge Maggie would normally refuse without serious coaxing.

The next level was a simple landing with a small circular window, the glass darkened by decades of salt grime. She hesitated there, catching her breath, then continued up the next stretch of steps.

She climbed higher, the walls closing in tighter as she went, her breath whistling in her throat. She knew it was probably her imagination—there was just as much oxygen here as there was on the lower level—but panic edged its way in. Her palm on the railing was slick with sweat.

"Mag—?" She paused her climbing and listened again. There it was—that incessant scritching, rhythmic and frantic. Now she could hear something else—the familiar, wet snuffling of her dog.

Lucy jogged up the remaining steps, the railing wobbling under the weight of her hand, her backpack bouncing. She followed her flashlight beam to the top floor, a narrow landing centered around the archaic, long-dead lamp. A chest-high wall circled the octagonal room. Above that, a cage of cast-iron bars left the lamp—and Lucy—open to the elements.

She inhaled, grateful for the fresh air, and peered through the bars at the shore below, at the park and town beyond. A wave of vertigo rocked her, and she put one hand on the cement wall until it passed.

She found Maggie on the other side of the lamp compartment and allowed herself to breathe. The dog was capable of launching herself over higher fences in pursuit of squirrels—and could squeeze through spaces half the width of these cast-iron bars—but up here, her canine escape artist was more preoccupied with digging.

Lucy trained her light on the dog and noted the faint whiff of oil. Maggie raked at the wooden compartment that housed the base of the massive lamp, her muzzle frothy. Her claws had made a surprising dent in the rotted wood, and a pile of dark shavings was growing beneath it on the floor.

Lucy remembered learning, years ago, that lighthouse operators used whale oil to keep their lamps burning bright. For most dogs, a trip to the beach wasn't complete without a full-body roll on a dead fish or crab carcass—the stinkier the better. The scent of whale oil would be just as alluring.

"No!" Her breathless protest was barely audible over the dog's crazed scratching, the hammering of Lucy's heart.

Maggie stopped digging for a moment—as though Lucy had caught her doing something naughty—but then she went back to it, panting and whimpering.

Lucy knelt beside her dog, flashlight in one hand. She painted the lamp compartment with the beam of light—up, down, side to side. On one side of the compartment, she saw the barely visible edges of a door, its seams swollen by rot and salt air, the hinges on the right side darkened by rust. She tried to imagine a purpose for such a compartment.

Storage? Security?

Another guess presented itself to Lucy: *Century-old secrets?*

"Wait, Maggie," Lucy ordered, but the dog sniffed around the edges of the small door, stopping only when Lucy made a feeble attempt to pry the door open with her fingernails. The door refused to budge.

Maggie lay down before it, her muzzle on her front paws.

Lucy considered her shovel, but it was far too bulky. She patted her back pocket. "Ah!"

She took her keychain out, then jammed the long end of her house key into the door crack. She worked it, side to side, grunting with the effort of prying. She prayed her key wouldn't break. Maggie watched with her head tilted, panting.

Lucy was about to give up when she heard a splintering sound—ancient wood giving way—and the edge of the door swelled outward just enough for her to wedge the fingers of her other hand behind it. She pulled, still working the key, and the door popped open. The squealing of the rusted hinge made Maggie jump to her feet.

"We did it!" Lucy breathed.

She shrank back, prepared for the stench of decay to waft out, but there was only a puff of ancient dust and a hint of stale air and mildew.

Maggie crawled forward on her belly, snuffling but cautious. Lucy was ready to grab her collar, but the dog sat up again. She stared into the open compartment and let loose with a plaintive *unk unk unk*.

"It's okay, girl." Her stomach knotted with the irony of her statement. There was nothing okay about any of this. Maggie's finely tuned sense of smell—and maybe some other superhuman sense—had zeroed in on something that Lucy had not.

Someone was entombed inside that cubby.

Lucy trained her flashlight on the gaping cubby and took mental inventory: an impressive network of cobwebs, inches of dust, scattered rodent droppings. She gasped when she saw what lay beyond that. A wooden box, smaller than a carry-on suitcase, but big enough—

—Big enough to serve as a small coffin?

Lucy sat back on her heels and cried out. She withdrew the flashlight and let the beam jitter on the floor. "I can't."

Maggie got to her feet and nudged her, then lapped at her hand, an attempt at reassurance.

Lucy stood up and looked out over the harbor, gripping the bars like a prisoner yearning for freedom. The moon shimmered on the bay below, and in the distance, she could see the town, the geometric silhouettes of houses against the night sky.

Her eyes settled on a distant house—the only one with a turret piercing the horizon. She imagined it as it was a hundred years ago, when young Aoife had soothed her crying baby with lullabies.

When the young mother stood at the turret window—after tiny Calum's death—had she found comfort in the steady glow at the top of this lighthouse? Or had it served as a terrible reminder of everything she'd lost?

Had it only pushed her deeper into darkness?

A gust of wind, tinged with salt and tidal mud, blew Lucy's hair back and sent a whirl of dead leaves skittering across the floor. She turned from the window, blinking back tears, and went back to the open compartment.

"Okay, Maggie. Let's finish what we started."

Lucy got on her hands and knees and lay the flashlight on its side, blasting the inside of the compartment with light. The dust had settled, but she held her breath and reached in while Maggie tried to jam her head into the opening.

"Easy, girl."

She'd expected the box to be heavy, or for the moldering wood to crumble beneath her hands, but it slid out easily, bringing another puff of dust with it.

Maggie inspected the lid with her snout, her frantic snorts sending up more dust. She backed up and sneezed, but Lucy barely noticed.

Now that she'd brushed a thick layer of dust from the wooden surface with her sleeve, she could make out the image carved on the lid. It was a dove—its bird body and posture almost identical to Ava's jeweled brooch.

The Latin word for dove is columba—but the Gaelic word for it . . .

"Calum!" Lucy spoke it aloud, prompting Maggie to utter a single, high-pitched bark. The dog seemed to be waiting for her next move, but Lucy felt rooted to the spot, her eyes dazed.

Her mind revolted—she hadn't signed up for any of this—but her gut knew this was what she had come for.

Twenty minutes later, Lucy and Maggie set off in the rowboat, bound for the opposite shore. The box with the dove carving occupied most of the rowboat's floor.

A quick inspection in the lighthouse had revealed the lid to be nailed shut, and for that, Lucy was grateful. It absolved her of any duty to remove the lid, and it had allowed her to shimmy it down the winding staircase without the fear of it popping off. She'd kept her eyes on the rickety steps and tried to ignore the hollow clinking inside the box during their clumsy descent.

Her mind danced around the morbid possibility that this was all that remained of someone loved and lost—but she refused to spend more than a few seconds with that thought.

Right now, she had a job to finish.

34

Lucy stopped to set the box down for the fifth time since they'd found the trail opening behind the Myrtle Street house.

She'd let Maggie off her leash the moment they'd entered the woods—juggling the leash, the shovel and the box was impossible—but the dog stayed close.

She had tucked the flashlight into Maggie's collar, a makeshift headlight that zig-zagged to every trailside shrub that caught the dog's attention. It was starting to make Lucy dizzy.

"Maggie, stay."

The dog sat down, the flashlight beam whitewashing the treetops.

Lucy sighed and rubbed her stiff fingers. She cursed herself for not having brought a wagon or a rope to fashion a sling of some sort. The box was no heavier than her fully loaded school backpack, but it was awkward as hell. Carrying it on the overgrown path was treacherous.

She turned to see how far into the woods they'd come and found she could no longer see the turret of the Myrtle Street house through the trees.

"It shouldn't be much farther," she whispered.

Her mind scrolled back to the night she'd sleepwalked this path, and she laughed out loud when the realization struck her. That night, she'd texted her location to Nate more than once. Finding the ancient gravesite would be as easy as searching the location on her phone and hitting GO.

Lucy retrieved her phone from her back pocket and powered it on. Her screen lit up with the time—it was already after midnight—and then a flurry of notifications came through, one after the other. There were six missed calls from her parents and two concerned texts from Nate.

Her eyes settled on a series of consecutive texts from 1-11, all of them bearing the same message: *You're running out of time.*

"Now you're timing me?" Lucy lowered her phone and snorted. "Maybe you should do your own dirty work!"

Maggie sprang up, her front paws hitting Lucy on the chest, an unspoken question: *You okay, boss?*

"Down, girl," Lucy said.

Maggie abandoned her and advanced down the trail several paces. The dog stopped, one front paw raised, the flashlight beam illuminating her cocked ears. The dog's erect posture meant only one thing: she'd heard something.

"What is it, Mag—"

Now Lucy heard it, too—a faint wisp of a song mingling with the rustling leaves. Not just any song—a lullaby.

Aoife's lullaby.

Lucy's skin crawled, an eruption of goosebumps from head to toe. She stood still, listening, but the singing had stopped.

Or maybe she'd just imagined it.

Another sound pierced the darkness—the *hoo-hoo-hoo* . . . *hoo-hoot* of a female great horned owl—and Lucy reminded herself to breathe.

She found her text message to Nate, the location she'd sent that night. She tapped it and waited for the directions to come up, the wheel spinning endlessly.

Lucy sighed. "Shit signal. Of course."

In the distance, the owl hooted again, her way of announcing her location to whoever might be interested. She envied that owl, the simplicity of its existence, driven only by instinct.

The directions loaded on her screen. She hit GO and saw that her destination was five minutes away by foot.

"Continue north for four hundred feet." The female voice of her GPS app was robotic but oddly reassuring.

She pocketed her phone and nodded. "Four hundred feet. Yes, ma'am."

Without warning, Maggie bolted down the path, the light disappearing with her.

"Wait!" Lucy fumbled to pick up the wooden box and the shovel. "Maggie!"

Her phone spoke again: "Proceed to the route."

The moon had lit their way across the harbor, but the forest was shrouded in darkness. Lucy made her way forward blindly, testing each step on the path as she went, the contents of the box jostling whenever she stumbled.

She turned a corner and spotted Maggie's collar light—which was suspiciously immobile—just as her phone announced: "You have arrived at your destination."

"Maggie?" she called out.

The dog lowered herself to the ground, the light bobbing with her. Lucy stopped as she realized Maggie's front paws were nestled against the partially exposed gravestone, the one marked *eun*.

Relief swelled inside Lucy's chest. "Good girl, Maggie."

She set the box on the ground, her back protesting, and retrieved the flashlight from beneath Maggie's collar. She swept the light across the leaf-littered ground, frantic.

Now that she was here—so close to finishing what she'd started—she wasn't sure how to proceed.

The cell phone in her back pocket rang, and she snatched it up, hopeful. When she saw it wasn't 1-11—calling with direct instructions about where to dig—her shoulders dropped.

It was her mom.

"No," she groaned. She considered silencing the call, but she knew her mom had already tracked her location. Ignoring the call would tip her mom over the edge.

She answered it, cringing. "Mom?"

"Lucille Grace McGowen!"

Maggie stared at Lucy, her ears standing at attention.

"What the hell are you doing in the woods at almost one o'clock in the morning? Have you lost your freaking mind?"

"Maggie got off the leash and went on a wild rabbit chase," Lucy lied. "Good news is I just found her. We're headed back now."

"Stay there!" Lucy could see Joanne in her mind's eye, pacing the length of the kitchen, hopped up on coffee. "I'm coming to get you in the car."

"Mom, no!" Lucy looked at the shovel beside her. It was going to take more than a few minutes to dig a hole big enough to accommodate the wooden box. "I could really use the exercise—"

"You've been gone for two hours!" She heard the rattle of her mom's car keys over the phone. "We're going to have a serious talk when I get you back home, Lucy."

Her mom hung up, and Lucy stared at Maggie, her fingertips tingling with adrenaline. She powered her phone off and prayed her mom hadn't saved her location.

"Let's get to work, girl."

She hoisted the shovel, made a calculated guess, and stabbed the ground with it. The surface was littered with stones and roots, but the coastal soil was sandy and gave way easily. She shoveled faster, encouraged by her progress. Maggie circled around her, panting, then joined in the effort, her claws tearing at the dirt.

Twenty minutes later, Lucy stepped back to swipe the sweat from her forehead and appraise the hole they'd dug.

"What do you think, Maggie? Tight fit?"

The dog dragged her muzzle along the depths of the hole—corner to corner—as though she was measuring it.

In the distance, a car door slammed.

Lucy lunged for the box and hefted it into the hole. She worked it around, side to side, grunting—no time for decorum or reverence or last words. She took up the shovel and began tossing soil back in, darkening the lid with the dove carved into it.

"Lucy!" Her dad's voice cut through the darkness, sending a jolt of fear through her. It was his all-business tone, the one reserved for major infractions.

Maggie perked up, then blasted down the path toward his voice.

"Shit!" Lucy fell onto her knees and began flinging dirt around the box, packing it in around the edges, smoothing it over the top. She found an evergreen bough on the ground and lay it over the freshly dug grave, a last-ditch effort at camouflage.

She would have a hard enough time explaining herself tonight, especially now that her knees were blackened by dirt and her hair was a tangled, sweaty mess. If her parents discovered the grave—the ancient one and the one she'd just dug beside it—it would be a nightmare.

"Maggie, come!" Joanne's flustered voice rang out. "Get back here!" There was a shrill sound—Jeremy's trademark whistle—and Lucy saw Maggie in her mind's eye, galloping circles around them, a frothing Tasmanian devil.

Maggie had turned out to be a valuable accomplice on this bizarre mission, and now she was buying Lucy time to get herself together.

She lobbed the shovel into the bushes, then tucked her work gloves and backpack behind a tangle of ferns. If she wanted her parents to swallow her dog walk story, she'd have to come back for her stuff later.

She powered her phone on again—she could claim a weak signal for the GPS darkness of the last half hour—then gasped when she saw the time displayed on her screen.

It was exactly 1:11 a.m.

"Lucy!" Jeremy's voice was closer now, and he sounded pissed. "Get your ass over here *right now!*"

Lucy shoved her phone into her back pocket and spared a quick glance at the ground, which would hopefully go ignored for another hundred years.

She waited for some otherworldly signal that her mission was complete, but she heard nothing but a chorus of crickets and the distant crunching of footsteps on the path.

"Coming!" she called. She took off down the path, smoothing her hair into a ponytail as she hurried, an apology taking shape in her mind.

When her foot connected with a massive root—the same one she'd carefully stepped over on the way in—she went down hard, her arms flailing. There was a sickening crunch as her head struck a boulder, and then a bolt of pain exploded from the bony ridge above her left eye.

She had a random, disjointed thought—*New Hampshire, the granite state*!—before she began her helpless descent into oblivion.

The last thing she heard before she lost consciousness was the heavy beating of wings, a swooping she felt in her core. It was so close it blew her hair back, away from the wet trickle of blood, and then it was gone.

35

The forest was awash with moonlight.

Or . . . was the sun coming up?

Lucy could see the pink glow through her eyelids, though she couldn't feel the warmth of it on her face. A shiver rippled through her body as she tried to identify the bird chirping nearby—a repetitive *meep-meep-meep* she had never heard before. She wondered if it was a mockingbird, trying out the newest addition to its repertoire.

"Lucy?"

She turned her head toward the sound of her dad's voice, a bittersweet mix of fear and gratitude causing her throat to tighten. If he was angry, she couldn't tell.

"Dad, I can explain." The words came out wrong, her tongue thick and uncooperative. Her head was still killing her, but her jaw—it throbbed as though she'd hit the ground face-first.

"Shhh," Jeremy said. Lucy felt a gentle pressure on

her arm, the warmth of his hand. "Take it easy, Goose. You're going to be fine now."

Lucy's eyes popped open, and her heart kicked into a gallop. How much did her dad know? Had he somehow found proof of her mission—or, worse yet—had she blabbed about it while she was out cold?

"Never trust a sleep-talker," she mumbled.

She squinted against the light and frowned. The source of that light wasn't the rising sun after all, and she wasn't lying on the forest floor. This light was fluorescent, and she was indoors. That rhythmic chirping wasn't a bird; it was the mechanical beeping of a monitor. She felt the pinch of the IV needle taped to the back of her hand, the tube that connected her to the stand beside her reclined seat.

She tried to speak again—*had she fallen so hard they'd rushed her to the hospital?*—but there was something soft and bulky packed into her mouth. She desperately wanted to spit it out.

"Keep that in, Lucy," another voice chimed in. A pony-tailed woman in scrubs came into her view, smiling. "You can take it out later today."

Lucy glared at the woman—she was vaguely familiar—then closed her eyes as a wave of nausea washed over her.

Her dad leaned in close, bringing the smell of his aftershave with him. "They said you'd probably be out of sorts for a day or two," he said. "You had a bad allergic reaction to the sedative, Goose. Had us pretty worried for a while there."

It came rushing back to her, all at once: the tooth extraction, the jellyfish undulating on the ceiling screen, all of it.

Except—that had all happened weeks ago.

Hadn't it?

She lay there, her mind clawing for the details of the past month. Those events were growing fuzzy and out-of-focus, like the remnants of a dream after waking.

"Maggie," she murmured. She felt a tear slide from the corner of her eye, felt her dad wipe it away.

"Who's Maggie?" he asked.

The female voice came back, and Lucy could hear the smile in it. "She'll probably say some pretty wacky things for the next few hours, and the epinephrine might have her feeling jittery, too."

Lucy heard her cell phone ding, but she was too weak to reach for it.

"That's probably your mom," Jeremy said. "She couldn't leave her open house, but these guys took great care of you until I could get here."

Lucy felt a sob rise up inside her, and her mouth trembled. "I want to go back," she cried.

She remembered this place—this version of things—but she couldn't remember who she was supposed to be here. She wasn't sure if she could go back to the old way.

The old Lucy.

She lay there, her chest heaving, while her dad dabbed at her eyes with a tissue.

"Shhh, I know, Goose," he whispered. "As soon as you're up for it, we'll get you home."

LUCY HESITATED AT THE FRONT DOOR TO TAKE A FEW DEEP breaths.

The drive from Dr. Nelson's office had left her a little queasy, and the sedative hangover was slow to lift. She felt emotionally fragile—like a glass figurine riddled with hairline fractures—and the prospect of not finding Maggie at the front door made her want to cry.

Her dad held the door open for her, a question in his eyes. He was still clutching the milkshake he'd ordered at The Cone Zone, but she hadn't touched it.

"Coming?"

"Sorry," she said. "Still a little woozy."

The entryway was devoid of all signs of canine presence—no water bowl and surrounding splatters, no leash hanging on the doorknob, no scattered chew toys. Lucy stood there, blinking with disbelief. She'd braced herself for the lack of a greeting—for the stillness—but she had forgotten how quiet the house had felt in this life.

The kitchen was empty, no crockpot smells or cooling baked goods, no fresh-cut flowers or bowl of fresh fruit on the counter. She wandered to the refrigerator and opened it—the tidy rows and cartons replaced by carryout leftovers—and her dad gave her a hopeful look.

"Hungry, Goose?" He held up the melting milkshake. "Doctor said you're on a soft diet for a few days."

Lucy attempted to smile, but the right half of her face was numb and uncooperative. "Maybe later."

Jeremy smiled. "Your mom texted me to see how your extraction went," he offered. "Said she'll be home in a couple of hours."

Lucy nodded and sank into a chair. Her jaw was starting to tingle, the first prickles of sensation returning since her procedure, but the rest of her felt strangely numb.

Her eyes welled with tears when she realized what had her feeling so anesthetized. It was grief——for her other self in her other life, for all the moments lived and now lost.

Gone, like they had never happened at all.

36

Lucy woke with a jolt.

It took a moment to get her bearings: she was in her bed, her eyes pinned to the peeling paint on the ceiling above her, her legs occupying the bottom half of her bed instead of a snoring boxer.

She pressed a hand to her jaw, which was still swollen from surgery. The ache in her lower gum pulsed with her heartbeat, but it felt manageable.

She reached for the cell phone on her nightstand and powered it on. She sat up when she saw the onslaught of text messages from Nate at the top of her notifications.

She held her breath as she opened his most recent text: *Hey, you okay? Texted your dad and he said you had an allergic reaction!!*

Lucy sighed. These words were from the other Nate Mills, the one who made tending to her feelings a full-time job. The one who had never met the real Lucy McGowen.

Those electric moments up on the catwalk, in the school hallway, backstage at the talent show—they felt like fantasy, muted and distant. Without tangible proof, Lucy wasn't sure she could trust them.

She texted him back, a pit in her stomach: *Yesterday was ugly. I'm okay now.*

In actuality, yesterday was a blur in her mind—the prequel to her resurrection as the authentic Lucy McGowen. There were things about the other life that she hadn't loved—her mom's helicopter parenting, her dad's indifference—but she missed her newfound courage and the freedom that went with it. She missed the contentment of being herself, of authenticity and truth, of living out in the open.

She missed her dog.

Most of all, she missed the opportunity to start over again with Nate—to see him with fresh eyes and an open heart, and to let him see her.

Nate's text came back: *I miss you. Are you up for a visit?*

She lowered her phone and closed her eyes. She missed the new Lucy, too.

She texted him a response: *I'm a swollen, cranky mess. Maybe tomorrow?*

Lucy listened for the sounds she'd woken up to for the past month: tick-tack of dog claws on the wooden floor, dishes clinking in the kitchen, her mom's off-key singing. The house was dead silent.

Nate's text zipped back within seconds: *Lunch date tomorrow?*

Lucy felt a nervous flutter in her rib cage. She'd been on a zillion lunch dates with Nate—before—so why did his suggestion feel like such a first?

Fair warning: I'm on an ice cream diet this week, she texted.

In her mind's eye, she saw his mouth curve into a lopsided grin—the same lips that had brushed hers backstage, setting a flurry of butterflies loose in her stomach.

I fully support that, he responded.

Lucy found Joanne downstairs in her office, the room the other version of her mom had used for sewing projects and reading and meditating.

The family photos and collectible books were missing from the bookshelf, replaced by a dusty arrangement of real estate awards and framed magazine articles. The coffee cup on the desk read *SOLD Is My Favorite Four-Letter Word.*

Joanne's back was erect, her fingers clattering over her laptop keyboard.

Lucy cleared her throat. "Morning, Joanne," she said.

Her mom spun her chair to the side. "Hey. You heading off to school?"

Lucy fought the urge to roll her eyes. "It's . . . Saturday."

Her mom chuckled, then turned back to her computer. "Ah, yes," she sighed. "I vaguely remember weekends."

The keyboard clicking resumed, but Lucy stood there,

mute, until her numbness lifted, revealing the truth beneath it. Resentment simmered there, hot and dangerous.

"My mouth feels better this morning," she announced. "If you were wondering."

Joanne spun around again, her eyebrows arched high. "That's great, Lucy. I told you—high pain tolerance runs in the family."

Lucy wondered what her mom would say if she knew what else ran in their family—shame and secrecy, and if you went back far enough, a propensity for murder.

She did an about-face and headed for the kitchen, the perfect comeback fizzling somewhere between her mind and her mouth. She hesitated long enough to read the note her dad had left on the kitchen table, along with two twenty-dollar bills: *Your mom asked me to leave cash for soft food. Back tomorrow morning!*

Lucy grabbed the money and headed for the front door. She knew very well that her mom had nothing to do with leaving the money—with anything that didn't involve real estate—and she felt salty with her dad for pretending otherwise.

She was sick of pretending to be something she wasn't. She was tired of the disconnection and loneliness of the status quo. Waiting for things to change wasn't good enough. She needed to write her own future, the same way she put lyrics to music.

She knew it wouldn't be easy. Doing Aoife's bidding had been difficult, but she'd pulled it off.

Unlike Aoife, Lucy had her whole life ahead of her.

She could fall back into her so-called comfort zone, or she could do whatever it took to bury the old Lucy—the version of herself that was silenced by shame and fear.

She could let herself be born again, once and for all.

37

Lucy expected to find 111 Myrtle Street restored to its refurbished state, but the sight of it shook her nonetheless.

The lawn and shrubs were neatly trimmed, the paint fresh, the Harbor Home Hunters sign in place. A lone brochure, probably dropped by an open house visitor, lay on the front porch, but the colorful balloons and OPEN HOUSE signboard were missing.

Her eyes wandered to the woods beyond the house, the forest path hidden by lush ferns. When she looked back at the house, it was a moment before she realized they were gone—the wooden figures in the windows, the carved gulls flanking the porch railings like sentries, even the ancient, spread-winged osprey at the top of the turret. The absence of those birds made her question her own sanity.

She made her way up the front steps to inspect the

railings and found their tops sanded and smooth, with no hint of Samuel Cormac's handiwork.

She ran her hands over them and frowned. "You existed," she whispered. "You mattered."

She started down the steps, dazed. She'd come here for validation, but she felt the malevolent tendrils of doubt worming their way in. She'd been telling herself that her time in that other life—Ava's desperate pleas, her own sleepwalking and transformation—had been more than an elaborate fever dream. Now she wasn't so sure.

Her cell phone dinged with a new text. She waited for the old feeling to come—to feel irritated or smothered by Nate checking in—but instead she felt hopeful. Starting over would not be easy, but she welcomed the opportunity.

The text wasn't from Nate after all.

It was from 1-11, the first message to find her since she'd returned to this stale version of reality.

Earlier, Lucy had tried to scroll back through her text history with 1-11, a.k.a. Aoife Cormac. It was gone, as absent as the rest of the text messages from that other life—the ones from Nate, Ella, Abby, her parents. Her cell phone had no record of any of it, and she feared it would be purged from her memory before long, too.

She opened the new text with a grateful sigh. "I'm not crazy."

The message consisted of two words: *It's unlocked.*

Lucy scanned the street, found it empty of cars and pedestrians, then went to the front door. The antique knob turned easily, and the door swung inward. The scent of cinnamon potpourri greeted her—Joanne's favorite open house trick—but the air beneath it was musty.

She closed the door behind her and looked around, her pulse throbbing at her temples. She was struck by the stillness in the house. There was nothing—no ticking clock, no humming refrigerator—to disturb the silence. It was as if the house was holding its breath, waiting for Lucy's next move.

Her phone chimed again, jangling her nerves.

Another message from 1-11, this one almost playful: *I left something for you upstairs.*

Lucy's eyes went to the staircase, its ornate railing still gleaming from a fresh coat of varnish. It twisted up into the shadows, where the halls and corners had once echoed with the sounds of a crying baby, the secrets of a forgotten family.

The sudden urge to bolt from the house rose up inside Lucy, but her curiosity was stronger. She started up the stairs, her heart knocking against her ribcage. She hated the thought of confronting the spirit's physical embodiment—the voiceless but fiery Ava—but she wasn't sure why. She'd done everything Aoife had asked of her.

The air on the second floor was stuffy and warm. Lucy walked the corridor, past the bedrooms on either side, her gaze on the door at the end of the hall. Instinct told her the narrow stairs to the third-floor turret were behind that door.

She followed the spiral staircase up, her footsteps echoing until she reached the octagonal room at the top.

Lucy exhaled, relieved to find the room empty. The walls were awash in golden light, the curtains still parted for the open house. The cleaning crew had missed the cobwebs criss-crossing the corners of the ceiling, their fine strands weighed down by years of dust.

She went to the window overlooking the woods. Beyond the treeline, the harbor glistened. The island lighthouse jutted from the rocks below, a benevolent totem against a brilliant sky. The arched lighthouse door was missing, a gaping hole exposed by a violent spring gust or a vandal.

Lucy furrowed her brows with a faint memory—something to do with that door—but it slipped away before she could examine it.

She blinked hard, and then she spotted it there, glinting on the windowsill. She picked it up and turned it over in her hand, just to be sure.

It was Ava's antique brooch, the turtle dove with the ruby eye.

Her fingers trembled as she released the delicate clasp and pinned it to the breast pocket of her denim jacket.

"You're welcome," she whispered.

She was already pulling the cell phone from her back pocket when it chimed with another text message from 1-11.

One last favor?

38

When Ms. Waters looked up from the circulation desk, her penciled-on eyebrows shot up.

"Lucy McGowen!" She lowered her reading glasses and smiled. "Long time, no see. To what do I owe the honor?"

There was something unnerving about the librarian's formal greeting. It was obvious that their recent interactions—before and during the *Hauntings* book signing—existed only in Lucy's memory.

She managed a smile. "A little birdie told me some guy is writing a book about haunted houses of New England."

Little birdie? Was that a Freudian slip or a nudge from the spiritual realm?

Lucy looked at her hands, flustered. "I heard the author might be interested in the old Myrtle Street house. Does that ring any bells?"

Ms. Waters puckered her lips and considered that.

"Huh. I like to think I have my finger on the pulse of all things literary, but I don't remember anything about that."

Lucy frowned. This was going to be harder than she'd expected.

Ms. Waters perked up. "What did you say the author's name was, dear?"

"Edgar March." Lucy was suddenly breathless with hope. "I think he lives in Boston, but I can't find any more than that online."

Ms. Waters disappeared beneath the circulation desk to rummage in the wastebasket. She resurfaced with an unopened envelope.

"Ah!" the librarian exclaimed. "This arrived yesterday, but I assumed it was junk mail."

Lucy stared at the return address on the envelope. "That's him."

Ms. Waters pried the envelope open with excruciating care while Lucy looked on. The librarian unfolded the handwritten request and read it silently, her lips moving.

She glanced up at Lucy and grinned. "Isn't that something? Here it is—his request to interview me and some other history buffs about the Myrtle Street house. It's his first book—says he's hoping to finish it by the end of the summer."

Lucy raised an eyebrow. "New Hampshire in autumn sounds like the perfect backdrop for a book signing."

The librarian nodded her approval. "Doesn't it?"

Lucy leaned in close. "Ms. Waters, I was actually hoping to contact the author, maybe pick his brain." She shrugged. "I've been thinking about starting a book club at school."

Ms. Waters nodded, her eyes huge behind her glasses. "Our Friends of the Library book club hasn't met in months. Perhaps I'll revive it with *Hauntings of New England*."

Lucy offered a bright smile. "Did the author include his email address in that letter?"

Ms. Waters handed the letter over and winked. "Ask him if he ever does book signings, dear. No one with a conscience would say no to a young reader."

Lucy pedaled her bike as if her life depended on it.

In her mind, she composed the email she was planning to send Edgar March.

When she spotted them, she braked hard, then straddled her bike before it could fall over. She dragged her forearm across her eyes and wondered if she was seeing a moving mirage—or if delayed hallucinations might be a side effect of yesterday's sedative.

"Hey!" It was Ella in the flesh, smiling as she jogged up the sidewalk toward her. "I've been to hell in a handbasket looking for you!"

Lucy let her bike collapse to the ground, then took a few cautious steps toward her friend. She wasn't alone—she had a leash wrapped around each wrist, one attached to her own dog, Rosie, the other stretched taut behind a straining brindle boxer.

Lucy sank to her knees, her eyes blurred with tears, and spread her arms wide.

The boxer launched into her, tongue lolling, stubby tail wagging. Lucy wrapped her arms around the dog's muscled neck and cried out.

"Look at that chemistry!" Ella beamed. "My mom's on a major fostering kick this week. She's got two more dogs at home, a guinea pig and a bearded dragon. Get this—she was on the phone with your mom just now and had her ninety-five percent talked into adopting." She doubled over to catch her breath. "This sweet girl here was on death row. Her name is—"

"Maggie," Lucy murmured. She smiled and let the boxer lap the tears from her cheeks.

Ella fixed her with an incredulous look. "How in holy Hades did you know that?"

Lucy shrugged. "Lucky guess?"

WHEN LUCY GOT HOME, SHE CREPT PAST HER MOM'S office.

She heard the telltale squeak of the office chair, the click of her mom's heels on the wooden floor. "That you, Lucy?"

Lucy stopped and turned. She squared her shoulders and braced herself for a lecture. "I swear I didn't put Ella's mom up to that phone call. The pet fostering is just her obsession of the week."

Joanne put a hand on her hip and shrugged. "I know."

Lucy looked for the razor edge in her mom's tone and couldn't find it. She scrolled through her cell phone pictures and held it up. "Speaking of dogs, I just ran into Ella walking one of them. She's pretty cute, huh?"

Joanne squinted at the phone. "She looks like a handful." She folded her arms and smiled. "Ella's mom did make an excellent point on the phone. She said boxers are fantastic guard dogs, and with your dad out of town half the time . . ."

Lucy stared at her mom. Was she actually considering it? After years of saying no to a pet of any kind? "Protective *and* loyal," she agreed.

Joanne narrowed her eyes and bent her head. Her mouth fell open. "What the——where the hell did you get that?"

Lucy followed her mom's eyes downward to the focus of her scrutiny——the brooch pinned to her pocket. "This?" She avoided her mom's penetrating gaze. "I . . . a friend gave it to me."

It wasn't a complete lie, but her mom looked skeptical.

"Jesus," Joanne said, leaning in closer. Lucy realized it was amazement——not anger——in her mom's eyes.

"You've seen one like it before?" she ventured.

Joanne frowned. "Not in person." She went to the bookshelf, then found what she was looking for. She held up the leather-bound book for Lucy to see.

"A Bible?" she asked.

Her mom leafed through the book, then found what she was looking for tucked between the pages.

She held up a yellowed photograph, then handed it to Lucy.

"Careful," she warned. "It's your dad's only copy."

Lucy studied the photo, her mouth agape. It was a reprint of the photo she'd unearthed in the basement heirloom chest—only in this one, the young subject wore a high-collared dress, a jeweled dove brooch pinned at her throat. In her arms, she held an infant in a lace christening gown. It was the same gown Lucy had left the basement with after her first sleepwalking episode.

Joanne reached for the photo, her face tight with concern, something Lucy wasn't used to seeing on her mom's face—at least, not *this* version of her.

"You okay, Lucy? You're shaking like a leaf."

Lucy found her voice. "I'm fine," she said. "Been a little off since yesterday."

Joanne tucked the photo back into the pages of the Bible. Her posture had changed in an instant, and Lucy could see that she was sliding back into work mode.

"The girl in the photo," she said. "Who is she?"

Joanne ran her hands through her hair and shrugged. "She goes back several generations on your dad's mother's side. One of his great aunts has been getting into genealogy and sent this copy to your dad about a month ago. Last name starts with a C, I think."

C, as in Cormac.

Lucy put a hand on the doorjamb to steady herself and lowered her eyes so her mom wouldn't see her shock.

Aoife Cormac hadn't chosen Lucy to do her bidding randomly. She had chosen her because she was family.

She considered asking her mom about the heirloom chest beneath the basement stairs, but somehow she already knew it wasn't there and never had been. Not in this life, anyway.

"Your dad's ancestors were Scottish immigrants," Joanne continued. "They settled in New England in the eighteen-hundreds. I guess we know who to thank for that auburn hair of yours, huh?"

Lucy forced a smile. "I guess so."

She wandered toward the stairs and was halfway up when her mom poked her head out of her office again.

"Hey, Luce? Maybe we can do a trial run with that boxer this weekend. Give her a chance to prove herself."

"Really? Thanks, Mom."

She cringed as soon as the word was out, but Joanne tilted her head as though she was trying the nickname on for size.

"Can't remember the last time you called me that," she finally said. "I don't hate it."

39

Lucy was in the kitchen, trying to decide if mac and cheese fell into the soft food category, when her dad came through the front door.

He wheeled his suitcase behind him, his other hand loosening his uniform tie. Jeremy wasted no time ditching his epaulettes and polyester pants for jeans and a T-shirt, and the furrow between his brows would disappear along with his uniform.

When he caught sight of Lucy, his face brightened. "Hey, Goose. How're you feeling?"

"Less like a chipmunk than yesterday," she said.

Jeremy fished his hand into his shirt pocket. "I almost forgot. Friend of yours dropped this off for you a few minutes ago."

Lucy blinked at him. "Really? Who?"

"Long, dark hair. Didn't catch her name."

Lucy went to the window and peered out, but there was no sign of anyone.

She took the envelope from her dad. "Did she . . . say anything?"

Jeremy shrugged as he worked his shirt buttons free. "Just that the two of you were working on a history project together. I invited her in, but she said she had a family obligation."

Lucy swallowed hard and let her fingers trace the sharp angles of the brooch pinned to her jacket.

It seemed she had somehow helped Ava find more than her long, lost child.

She'd also helped her find her voice again.

Lucy retreated to her bedroom, but she wasn't prepared for what she found on those pages.

The paper was white and the ink was fresh, but it read like an old diary entry, the words plucked from a bygone era. She sat on her bed and read it, swiping the tears from her face before they could fall onto the pages and smear the writing.

She had to remind herself that this was the ancient confession of her ancestor, Aoife Cormac, who shared a forbidden love with a commoner, the young son of the lighthouse keeper. Aoife's father had put a stop to their scandalous courtship—but he could not prevent baby Calum from coming into the world.

What Aoife had felt for her baby—the illegitimate son her parents refused to accept—was a fierce and protective love. Her lullabies were meant to soothe the infant's tears, but they also served as proof that he existed, and that he deserved a place in the world.

Just days after baby Calum was born, the unimaginable had happened. The baby went missing, but fate had nothing to do with his death. His own grandfather, Samuel Cormac, suffocated him in his cradle. He placed his small, lifeless body in the box with the bird carving, then allowed the cold harbor to swallow him, with only the full moon as witness.

Aoife's father had claimed the infant was a victim of kidnapping, and her parents never spoke another word about him. Aoife and her baby had been victims of familial pride, the kind that values status and reputation above all else.

A week later, the box holding the tiny body of Calum washed up on the rocky shores of the island across the harbor. The young lighthouse keeper discovered it, and he gave his son a secret burial inside the lighthouse. He buried his grief—and his hopes of a future with Aoife—along with him.

"They killed him." Lucy buried her face in her hands. "And in the process, they killed you, too. I'm so sorry."

Lucy curled up on her bed, her knees drawn to her chest, her body heaving with the sobs she couldn't allow. After a while she dozed off, the tears drying on her face, Ava's confession tucked under her pillow.

She dreamed, a feverish swirl of borrowed memories. Secret, forbidden love. Swollen belly, heart heavy with shame and fear. A mother's love—raw and ultimately lethal, but powerful enough to endure long after death.

When she woke, Lucy took a deep breath and opened her laptop to compose an email to Edgar March. She told him everything—that the ghost haunting the Myrtle Street house was a young mother in mourning, that her child's life had been snuffed out to preserve the family name, that Aoife had died of a broken heart, her ghostly lullabies a cry for help. She told the author that she knew, firsthand, that Aoife and Calum were resting now, together.

After she hit send, regret seized her.

Why should the author believe the unsolicited ramblings of a complete stranger? What if he called her out as some kind of loon—or, worse yet, what if her claims caused him to remove the Myrtle House story from his book altogether?

She started to write another email to the author—an apology or a retraction—when his response appeared in her inbox.

Miss McGowen:

Your email was quite fortuitous. I happen to be in the final stages of editing my manuscript, Hauntings of New England, which I was planning to submit to my editor tomorrow. The insight and details you have provided are absolutely priceless, and thanks to you, my chapter on the Myrtle Street house will be more complete and more interesting. I hope to make Portsmouth one of the stops on my New England book tour, and I would be happy to meet (and thank) you in person. I am truly grateful for your timely intervention.

Sincerely, Edgar March.

. . .

AN HOUR LATER, LUCY SAT ON TOP OF THE PICNIC TABLE at the park, her face turned up to the sun.

Aside from a pair of mallard ducks, she had the park to herself. She recognized the male duck, the small patch of missing feathers on his shimmering, green head. His mate crouched in the weeds nearby, a devoted mother protecting her nest. Lucy wished she could offer the mallards some reassurance; she'd glimpsed their future—five healthy ducklings—in that other life.

She thought about the mallard's bond, about the concept of happily ever after. She'd seen both sides—before and after—and now she was somewhere in between.

Somewhere new.

A car pulled into the gravel parking lot, and Lucy felt her pulse quicken. She let her attention drift to the lighthouse across the harbor—just as Aoife Cormac had done more than a century ago. She wondered if that lighthouse—where the keeper of the lamp and Aoife's heart had resided—felt more like home than 111 Myrtle Street.

Lucy heard footsteps approaching, and she smiled before he came into view. It was the same Nate Mills from before—eyes crinkling at the edges, hands thrust into his pockets, head ducked.

She met his shy gaze, familiar but new, and her core lit up with an electric zing.

"Hey, there she is." His voice wobbled with an effort to sound casual. "Worth the wait, as always."

"Hey." Lucy grinned. She knew he was referring to

the last two days, during which she'd gone silent, but she hadn't seen this version of Nate in weeks. Now she felt like she was seeing him with fresh eyes.

But Nate hadn't changed—*she* had.

He approached slowly, as though he was afraid to spook her. "How're you feeling?"

Lucy pressed a hand to her cheek. "Better than I look, I'm guessing."

Nate stared at her for a long moment, then shook his head. "You look great."

Lucy cleared her throat and looked away, her heartbeat in her throat. "I'm sorry if I've seemed distant lately," she said. "I've been dealing with some heavy stuff."

Nate reached out, then twined his fingers between hers. "No need to apologize, Lucy. And if you ever need to talk—about anything—I'm right here."

Lucy nodded. She had seen some major differences between this life and the other one—some of them beyond rational explanation—but Nate had remained constant and true.

"I know you are," she said.

Nate's eyes dropped to the guitar on the picnic table, and the notebook beside it—the one labeled *lyrics.*

He met her eyes, intrigued. "What's all this?"

Lucy looked away, blushing. Once she revealed this part of herself to him—to the world—there was no turning back. Hiding her passion for singing and songwriting had been easier, in a way. Safer.

A sound pierced the silence—the shrill *cheer-cheer-cheer*

of a nearby cardinal. She spotted it in the low branches of a birch tree, a female. It twitched its head, then flew away.

Lucy looked at Nate, her mind made up. Safety was overrated. If she was brave enough to reveal someone else's truth—even if it was a hundred years late—she could speak her own truth.

"I'm sorry," she whispered.

He raised his eyebrows at that. "For what?"

She reached for her guitar. "I haven't been totally honest with you."

He released her hand, crestfallen, and wiped his palm on his jeans. When she reclaimed his hand and squeezed it, he looked surprised.

"I'm Lucy McGowen . . . and I love to sing."

Nate fluttered his eyes at her, a smile tugging at the corners of his mouth. "Really?"

"Sometimes, when I'm alone in my room, I write my own music. I've been doing it for years."

"Seriously?" Nate's smile was incredulous. "That's really cool."

Lucy returned his smile. The confession had lifted a weight from her chest. "Thanks."

Nate slid his hand along the neck of the guitar, his face reverent. "Would you believe I've been thinking about taking guitar lessons myself?"

Lucy bobbed her head. "I have a strong feeling you're a natural."

He stared at her for a long moment, his hazel eyes

serious. He brushed her auburn hair out of her face, then bent to kiss her. They'd kissed countless times before, technically, but her stomach dropped as though they were careening into uncharted territory. She supposed they were, in a way.

He pulled back, his breath warm and shivery on her skin, then pressed his forehead to hers. "I don't know why, Luce, but you seem different."

She closed her eyes, and then she heard it again in the distance—the exuberant call of a mother cardinal reunited with her fledglings.

It occurred to her then—the reason behind her fascination with birds. They were ancient, evolved from theropod dinosaurs, but they were constantly reinventing themselves. Endlessly adapting but bound by absolutely nothing—not even gravity.

Lucy thought humans could learn a lot from birds.

She tilted her chin up to look into Nate's eyes. "You seem different, too," she said. "But in a good way. Maybe we're all just reinventing ourselves, little by little."

Nate grinned. "I like that." He reached for the guitar, a question on his face. "What are the chances I could get you to sing something for me?"

The old Lucy would have backed away—might have even been brought to tears by such a challenge—but that girl was history.

Lucy took the guitar from Nate and smiled. "I thought you'd never ask."

~

CHECK OUT *SYNCHRONICITY (BOOK 1 IN THE GEMINAE Duology) and SALVATION (Book 2 in The Geminae Duology),* both available in paperback on Amazon and in ebook at Amazon, Kobo, Barnes & Noble, Google Play and other ebook retailers.

ALSO BY LYNETTE DEVRIES

Book Two of The Geminae Duology

Book One of The Geminae Duology

ABOUT THE AUTHOR

Lynette DeVries is the author of *OtherLife*, as well as *Synchronicity* and *Salvation, Books 1 & 2 of The Geminae Duology*. She has enjoyed writing since early childhood, when a manual typewriter tucked under the Christmas tree inspired her to churn out mysteries and choose-your-own-adventure books. She has written for television, radio, advertising, newspapers, and magazines—but she is happiest when she is writing fiction. Lynette lives with her husband, two daughters, and two sloppy dogs in Florida.

Visit her at www.authorlynettedevries.com, or follow her on Facebook, Instagram or Twitter.

Made in the USA
Coppell, TX
16 March 2021